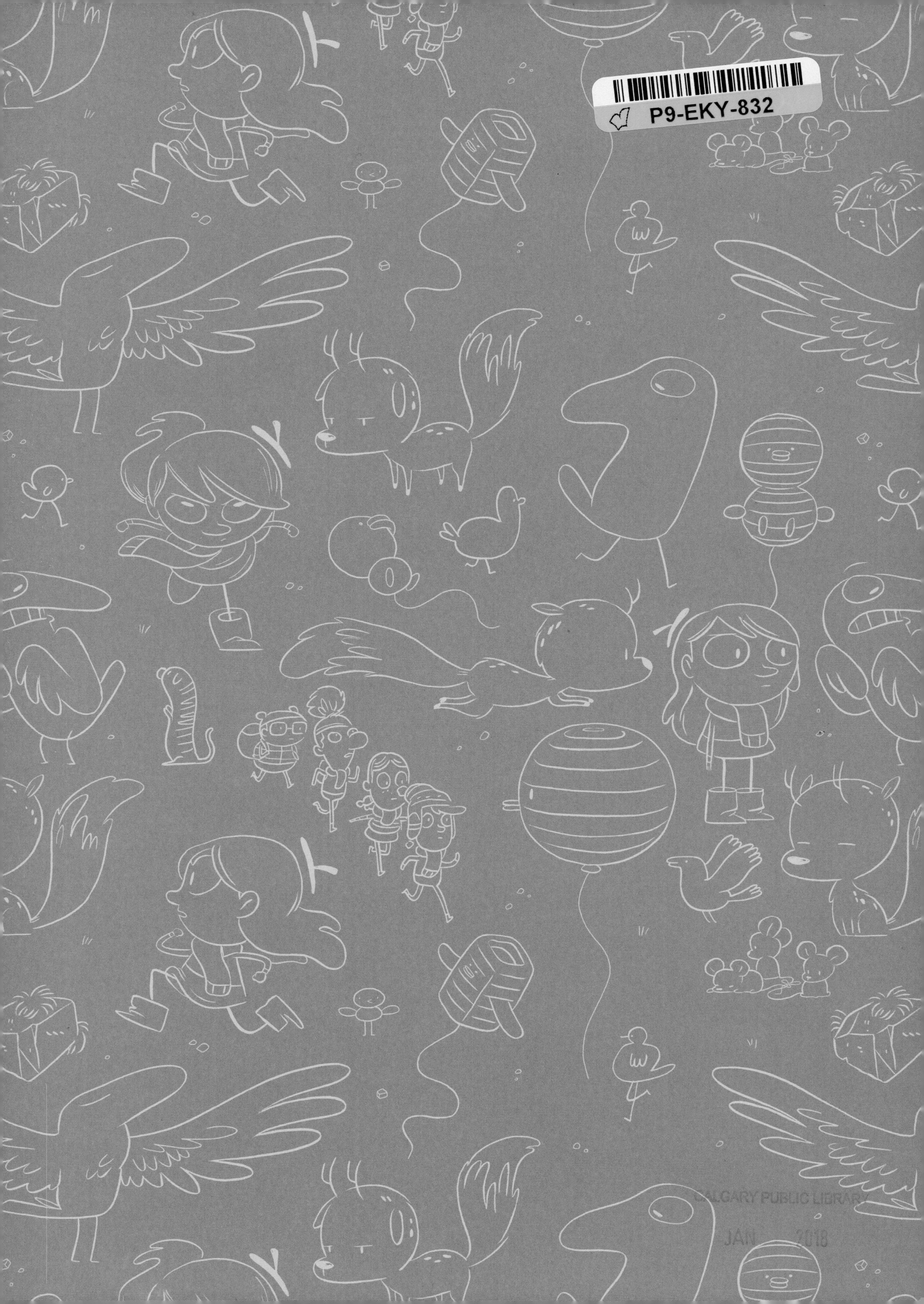

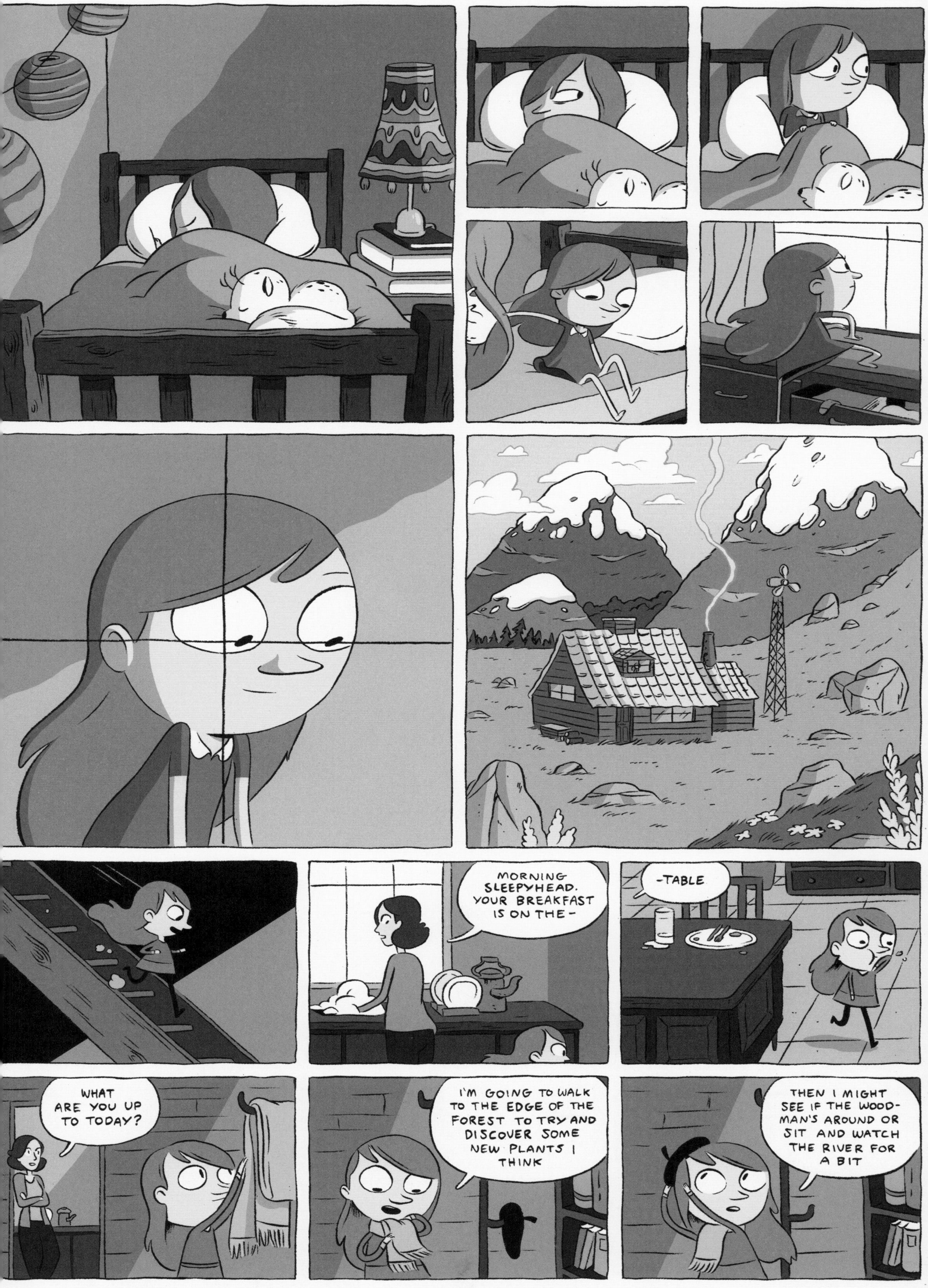
MORNING SLEEPYHEAD. YOUR BREAKFAST IS ON THE-
-TABLE
WHAT ARE YOU UP TO TODAY?
I'M GOING TO WALK TO THE EDGE OF THE FOREST TO TRY AND DISCOVER SOME NEW PLANTS I THINK
THEN I MIGHT SEE IF THE WOOD-MAN'S AROUND OR SIT AND WATCH THE RIVER FOR A BIT

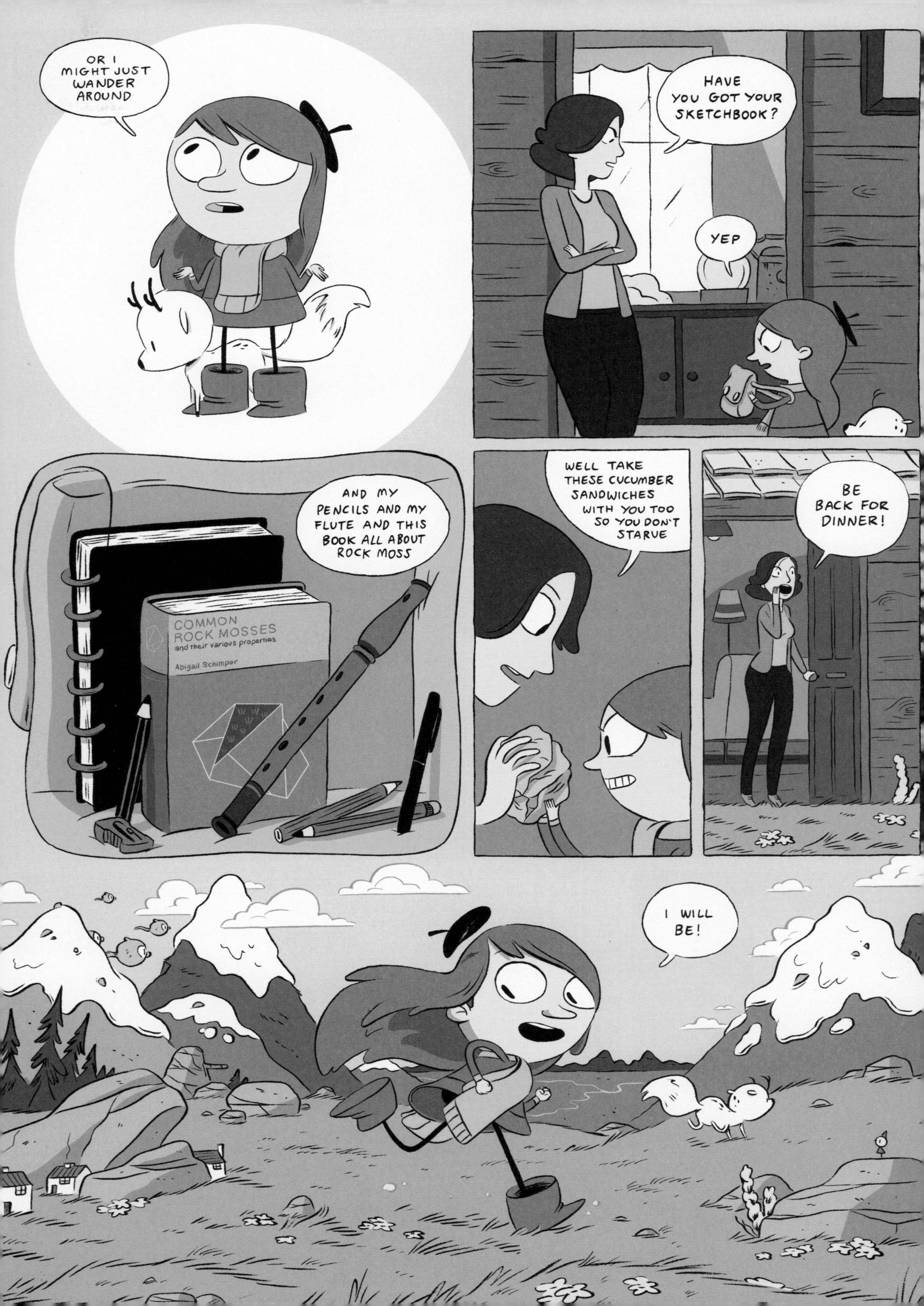
OR I MIGHT JUST WANDER AROUND
HAVE YOU GOT YOUR SKETCHBOOK?
YEP
AND MY PENCILS AND MY FLUTE AND THIS BOOK ALL ABOUT ROCK MOSS
COMMON ROCK MOSSES
and their various properties
Abigail Schimper
WELL TAKE THESE CUCUMBER SANDWICHES WITH YOU TOO SO YOU DON'T STARVE
BE BACK FOR DINNER!
I WILL BE!

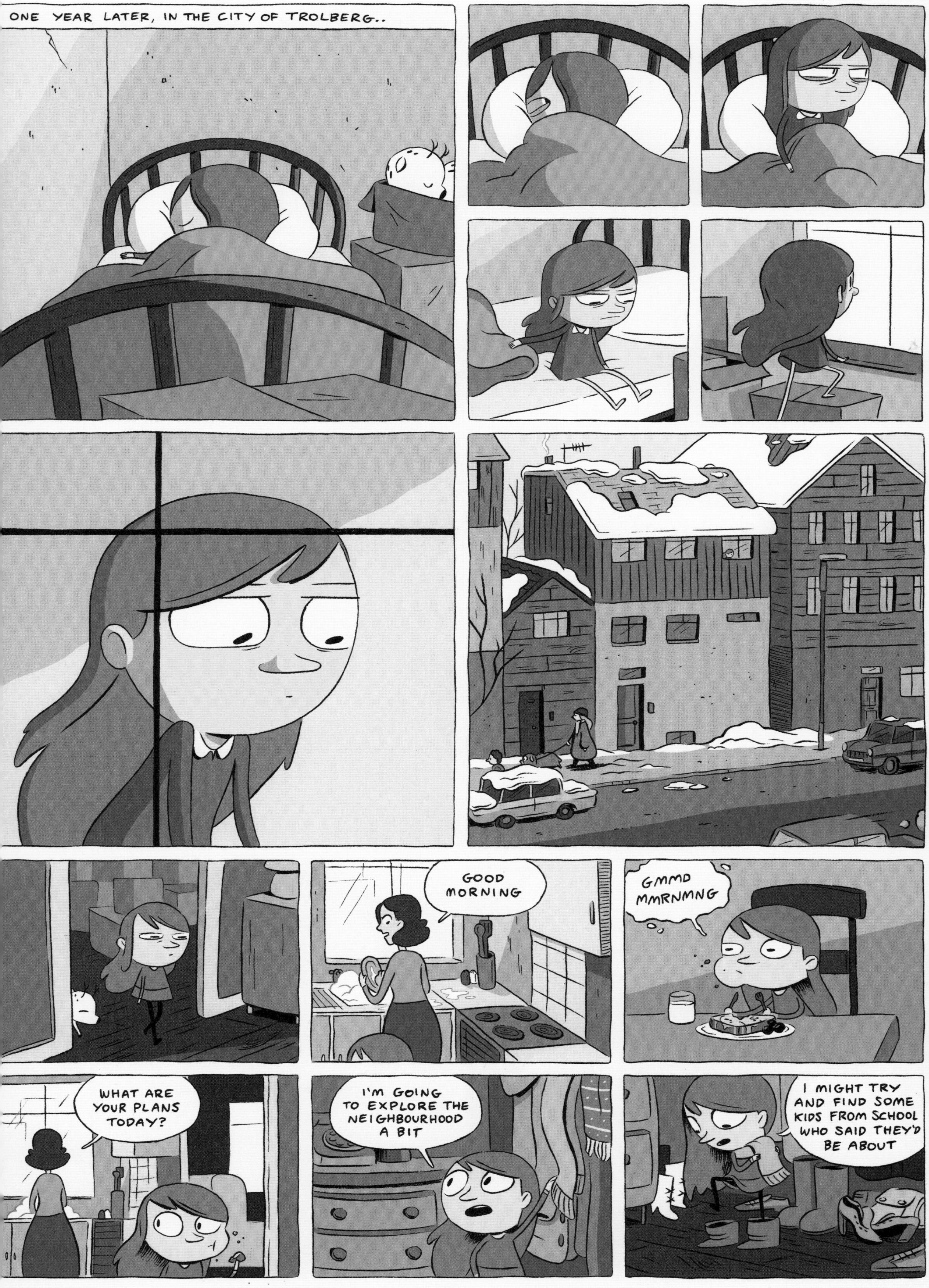
ONE YEAR LATER, IN THE CITY OF TROLBERG..
GOOD MORNING
GMMD MMRNMNG
WHAT ARE YOUR PLANS TODAY?
I'M GOING TO EXPLORE THE NEIGHBOURHOOD A BIT
I MIGHT TRY AND FIND SOME KIDS FROM SCHOOL WHO SAID THEY'D BE ABOUT

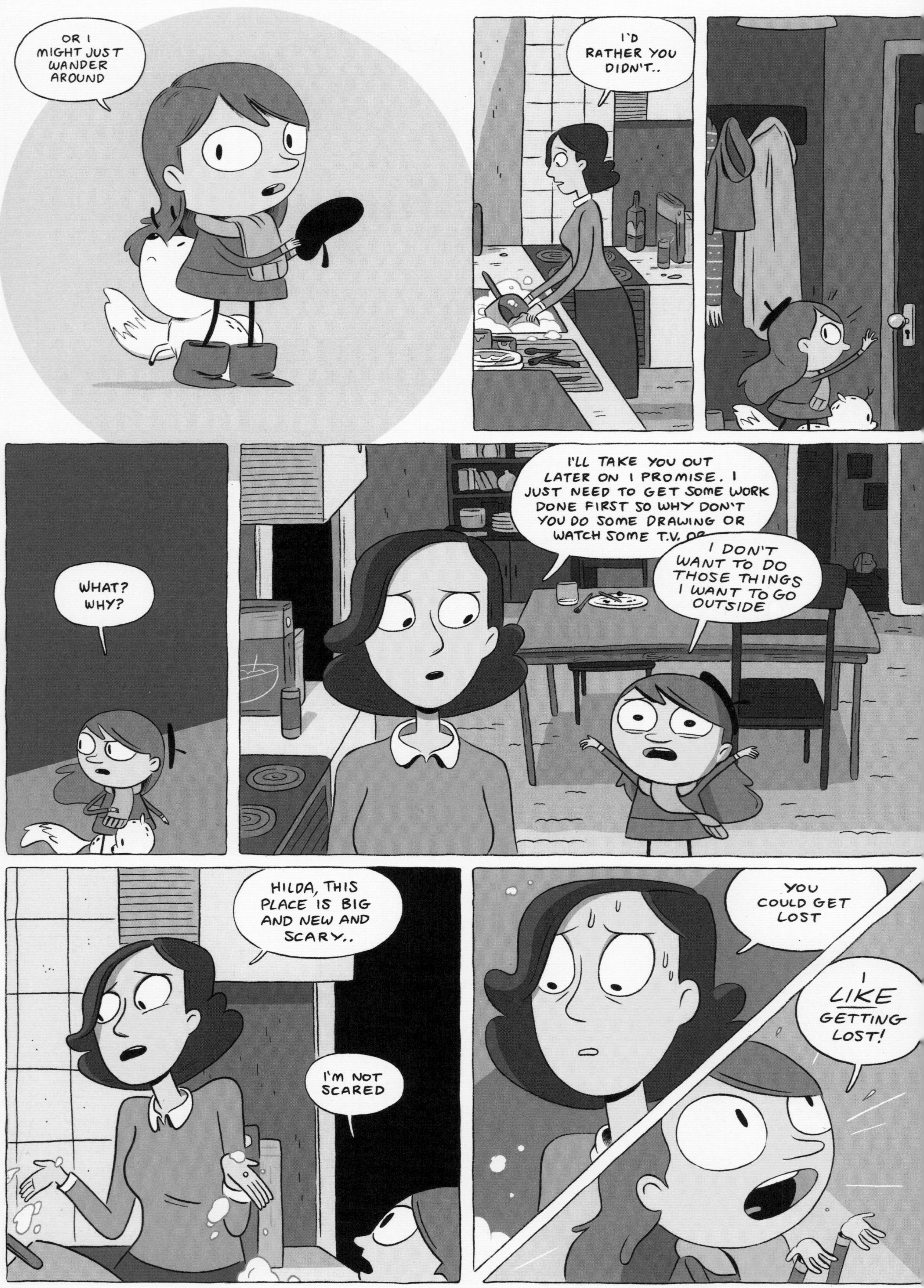
OR I MIGHT JUST WANDER AROUND
I'D RATHER YOU DIDN'T..
WHAT? WHY?
I'LL TAKE YOU OUT LATER ON I PROMISE. I JUST NEED TO GET SOME WORK DONE FIRST SO WHY DON'T YOU DO SOME DRAWING OR WATCH SOME T.V. OR
I DON'T WANT TO DO THOSE THINGS I WANT TO GO OUTSIDE
HILDA, THIS PLACE IS BIG AND NEW AND SCARY..
I'M NOT SCARED
YOU COULD GET LOST
I LIKE GETTING LOST!

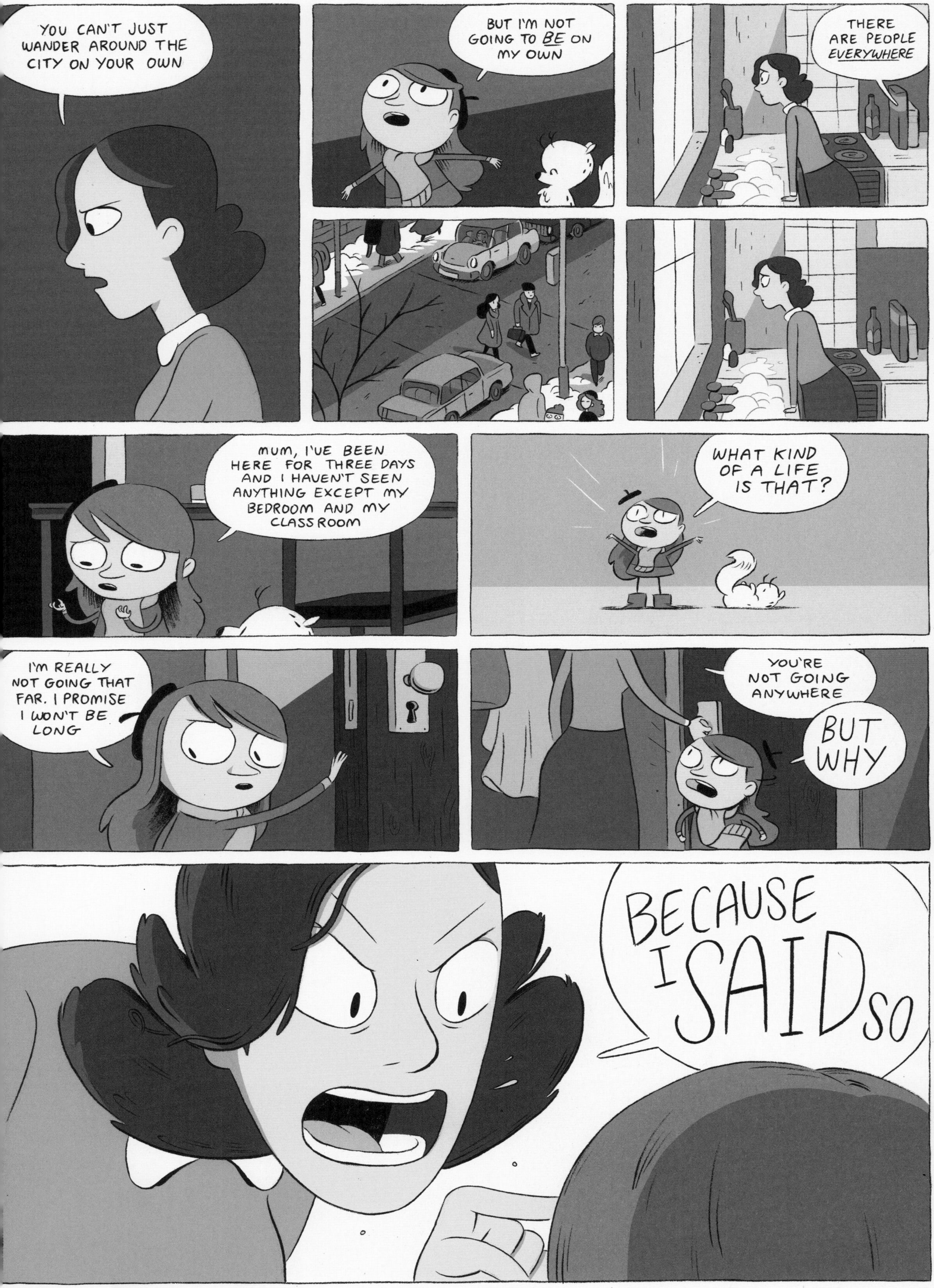
YOU CAN'T JUST WANDER AROUND THE CITY ON YOUR OWN
BUT I'M NOT GOING TO BE ON MY OWN
THERE ARE PEOPLE EVERYWHERE
MUM, I'VE BEEN HERE FOR THREE DAYS AND I HAVEN'T SEEN ANYTHING EXCEPT MY BEDROOM AND MY CLASSROOM
WHAT KIND OF A LIFE IS THAT?
I'M REALLY NOT GOING THAT FAR. I PROMISE I WON'T BE LONG
YOU'RE NOT GOING ANYWHERE
BUT WHY
BECAUSE I SAID SO

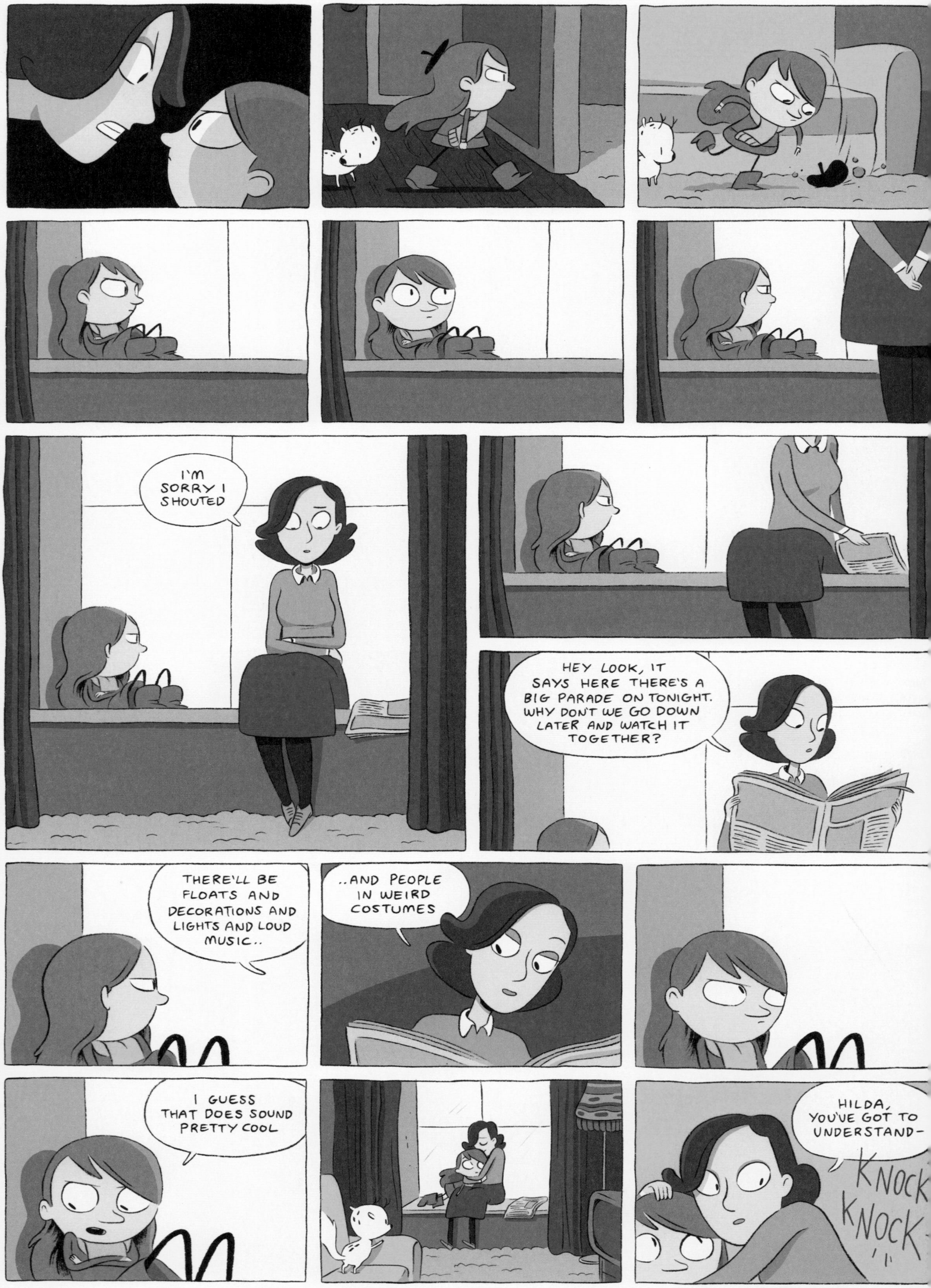
I'M SORRY I SHOUTED
HEY LOOK, IT SAYS HERE THERE'S A BIG PARADE ON TONIGHT. WHY DON'T WE GO DOWN LATER AND WATCH IT TOGETHER?
THERE'LL BE FLOATS AND DECORATIONS AND LIGHTS AND LOUD MUSIC..
..AND PEOPLE IN WEIRD COSTUMES
I GUESS THAT DOES SOUND PRETTY COOL
HILDA, YOU'VE GOT TO UNDERSTAND-
KNOCK KNOCK

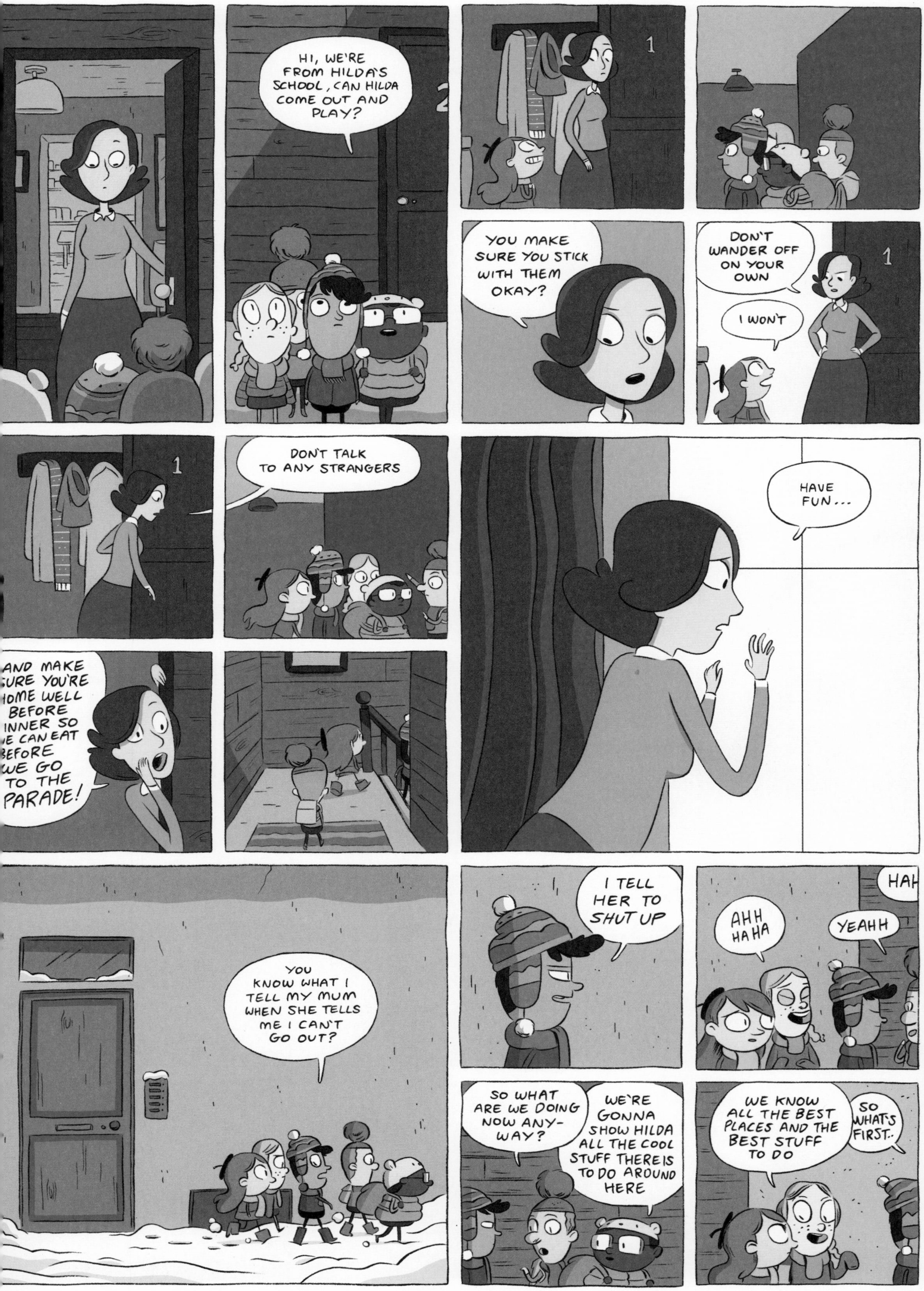
HI, WE'RE FROM HILDA'S SCHOOL, CAN HILDA COME OUT AND PLAY?
YOU MAKE SURE YOU STICK WITH THEM OKAY?
DON'T WANDER OFF ON YOUR OWN
I WON'T
DON'T TALK TO ANY STRANGERS
AND MAKE SURE YOU'RE HOME WELL BEFORE DINNER SO WE CAN EAT BEFORE WE GO TO THE PARADE!
HAVE FUN...
YOU KNOW WHAT I TELL MY MUM WHEN SHE TELLS ME I CAN'T GO OUT?
I TELL HER TO SHUT UP
AHH HAHA
YEAHH
HAH
SO WHAT ARE WE DOING NOW ANY-WAY?
WE'RE GONNA SHOW HILDA ALL THE COOL STUFF THERE IS TO DO AROUND HERE
WE KNOW ALL THE BEST PLACES AND THE BEST STUFF TO DO
SO WHAT'S FIRST..

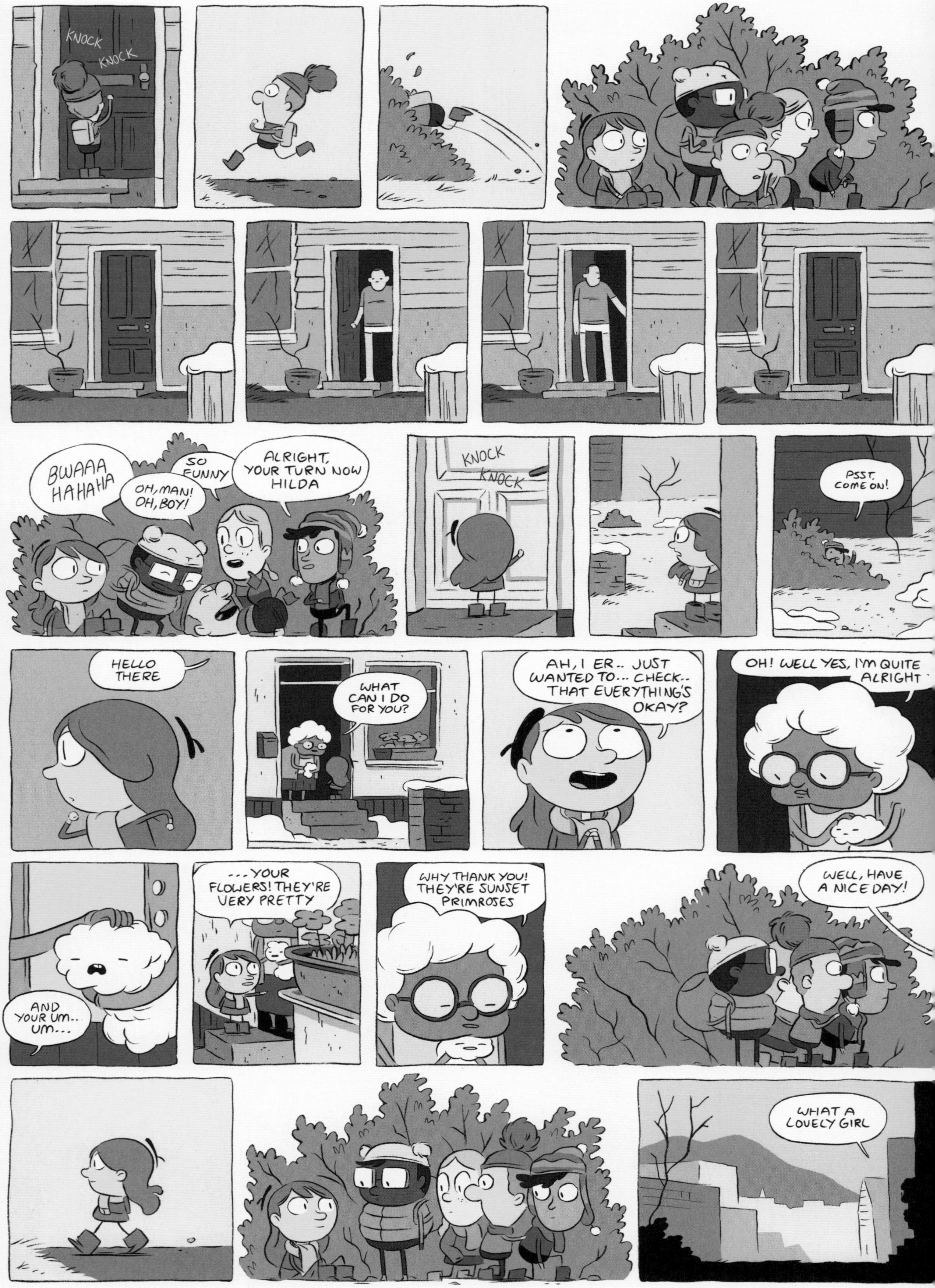
KNOCK
KNOCK
BWAAA HAHAHA
OH, MAN! OH, BOY!
SO FUNNY
ALRIGHT, YOUR TURN NOW HILDA
KNOCK
KNOCK
PSST. COME ON!
HELLO THERE
WHAT CAN I DO FOR YOU?
AH, I ER.. JUST WANTED TO... CHECK.. THAT EVERYTHING'S OKAY?
OH! WELL YES, I'M QUITE ALRIGHT
AND YOUR UM.. UM...
...YOUR FLOWERS! THEY'RE VERY PRETTY
WHY THANK YOU! THEY'RE SUNSET PRIMROSES
WELL, HAVE A NICE DAY!
WHAT A LOVELY GIRL

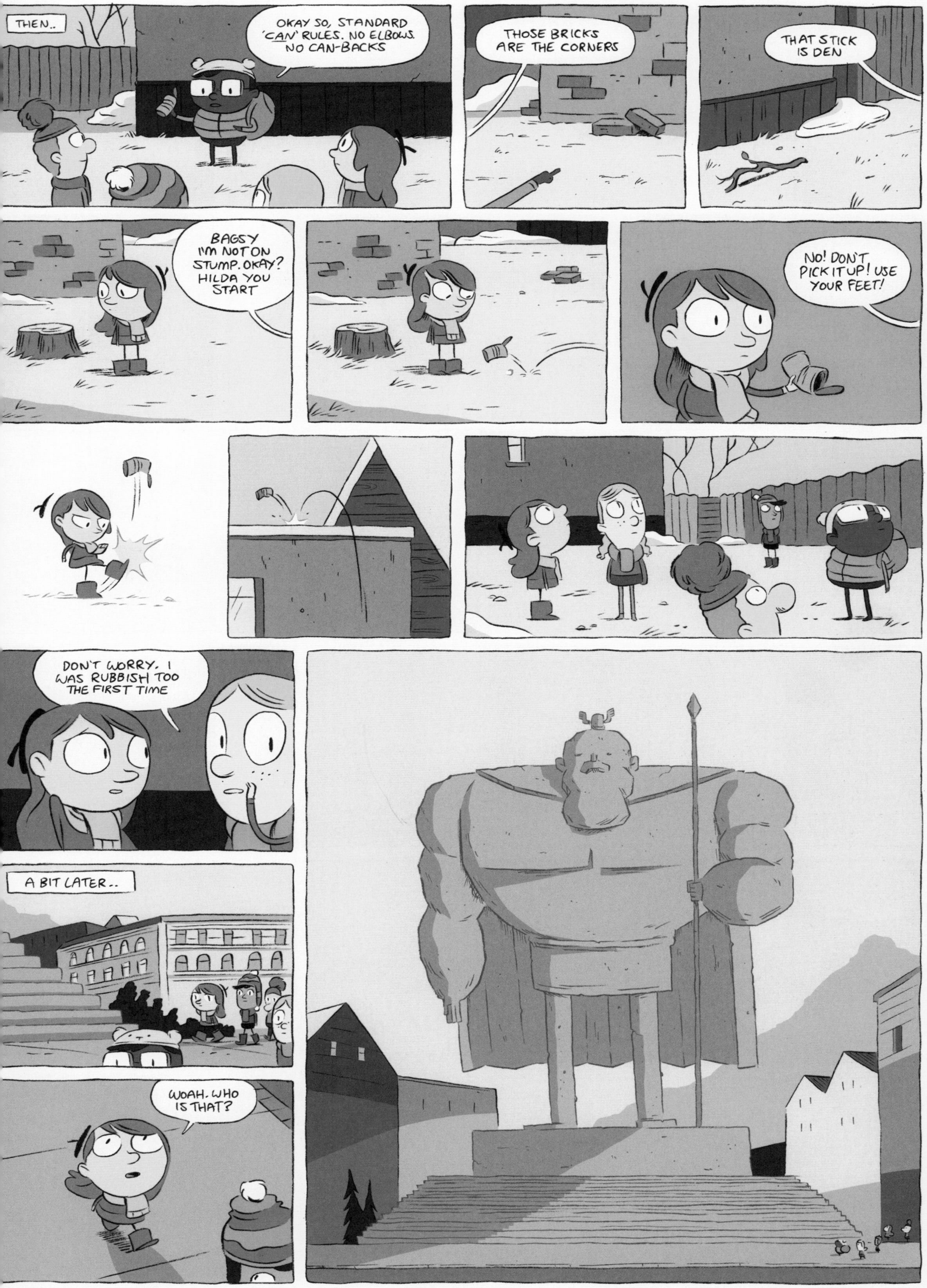
THEN..
OKAY SO, STANDARD 'CAN' RULES. NO ELBOWS. NO CAN-BACKS
THOSE BRICKS ARE THE CORNERS
THAT STICK IS DEN
BAGSY I'M NOT ON STUMP. OKAY? HILDA YOU START
NO! DON'T PICK IT UP! USE YOUR FEET!
DON'T WORRY. I WAS RUBBISH TOO THE FIRST TIME
A BIT LATER..
WOAH. WHO IS THAT?

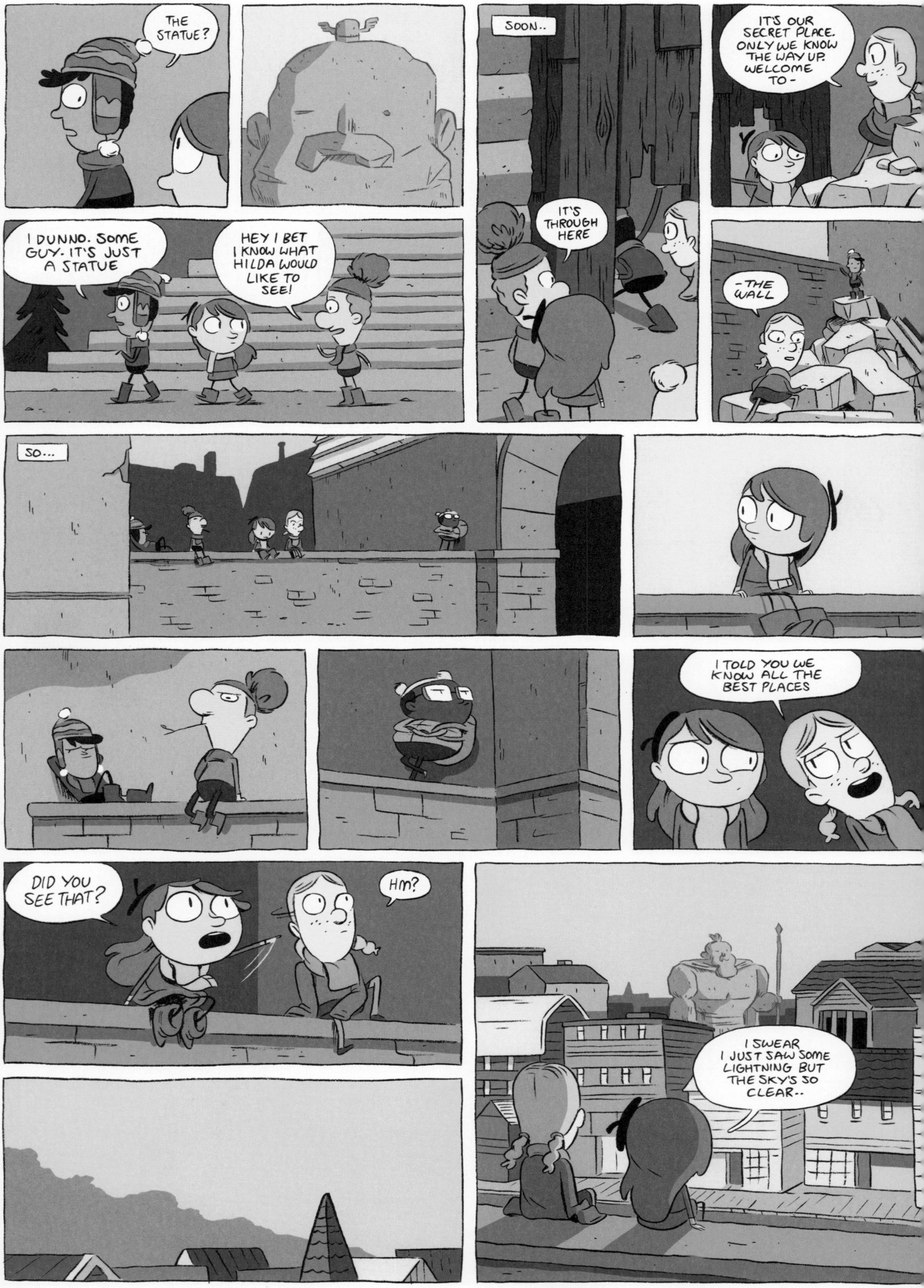
THE STATUE?
SOON..
IT'S OUR SECRET PLACE. ONLY WE KNOW THE WAY UP. WELCOME TO-
I DUNNO. SOME GUY- IT'S JUST A STATUE
HEY I BET I KNOW WHAT HILDA WOULD LIKE TO SEE!
IT'S THROUGH HERE
-THE WALL
SO...
I TOLD YOU WE KNOW ALL THE BEST PLACES
DID YOU SEE THAT?
Hm?
I SWEAR I JUST SAW SOME LIGHTNING BUT THE SKY'S SO CLEAR..

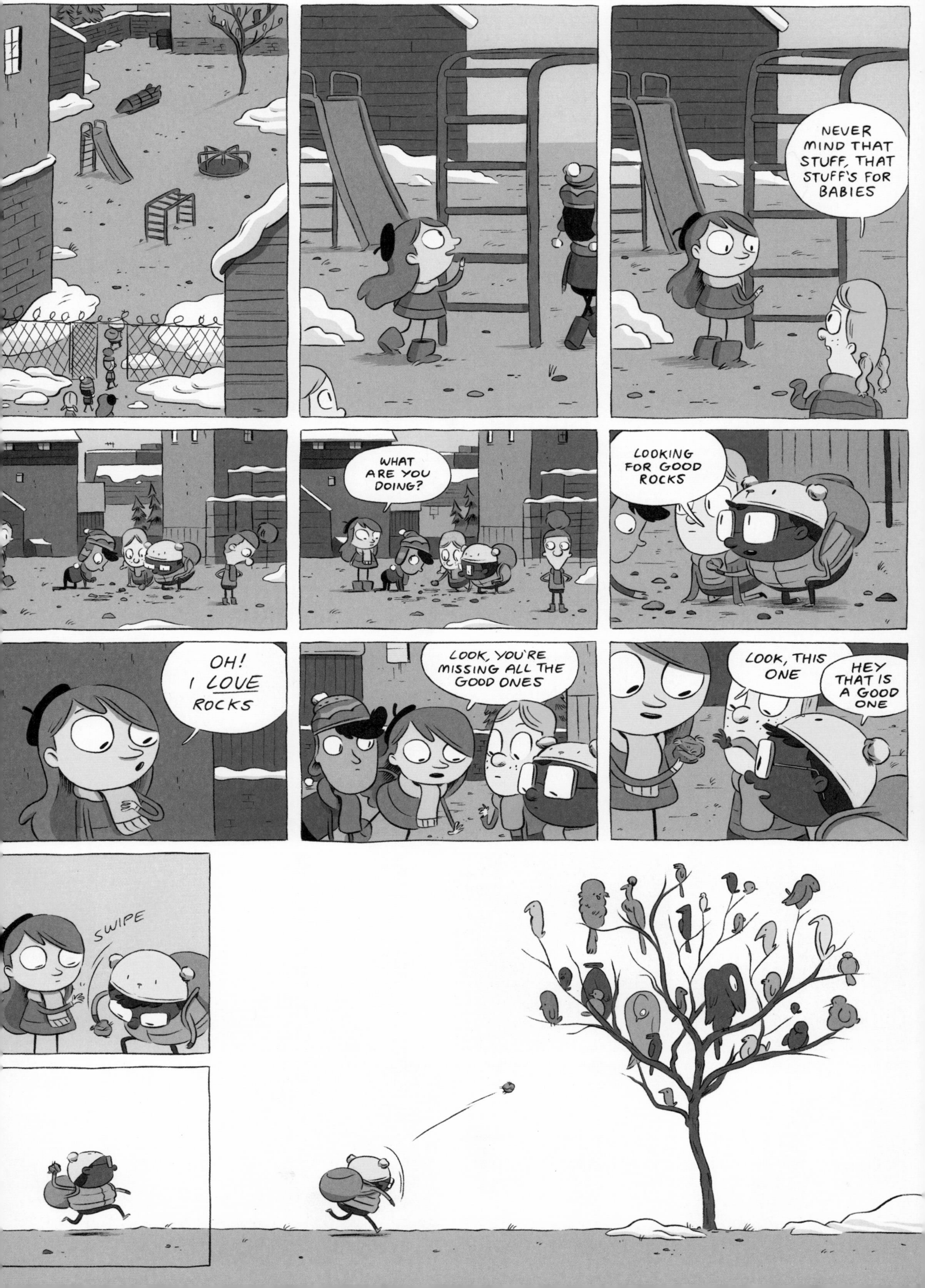

NEVER MIND THAT STUFF, THAT STUFF'S FOR BABIES
WHAT ARE YOU DOING?
LOOKING FOR GOOD ROCKS
OH! I LOVE ROCKS
LOOK, YOU'RE MISSING ALL THE GOOD ONES
LOOK, THIS ONE
HEY THAT IS A GOOD ONE
SWIPE

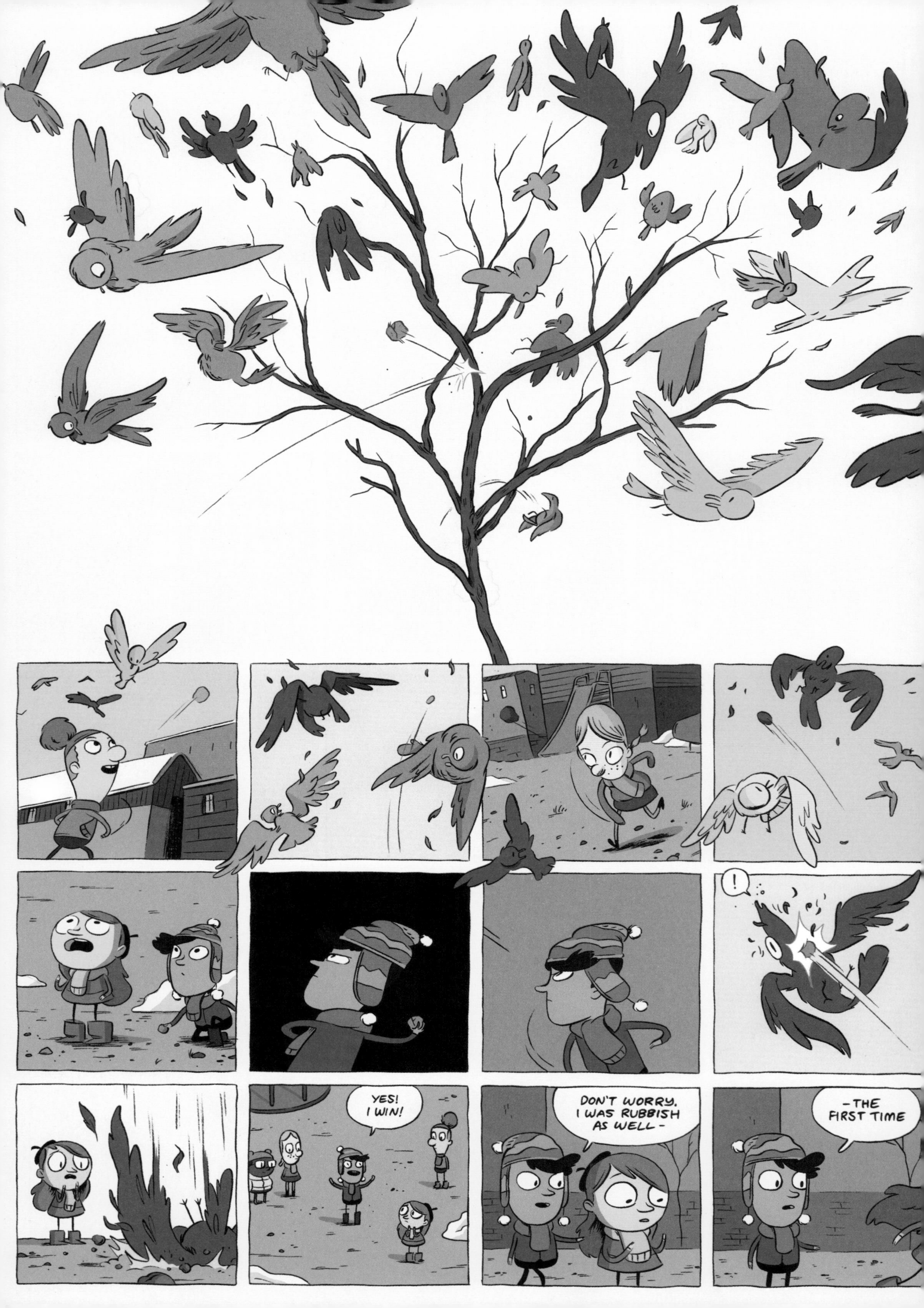
!
YES! I WIN!
DON'T WORRY. I WAS RUBBISH AS WELL -
- THE FIRST TIME

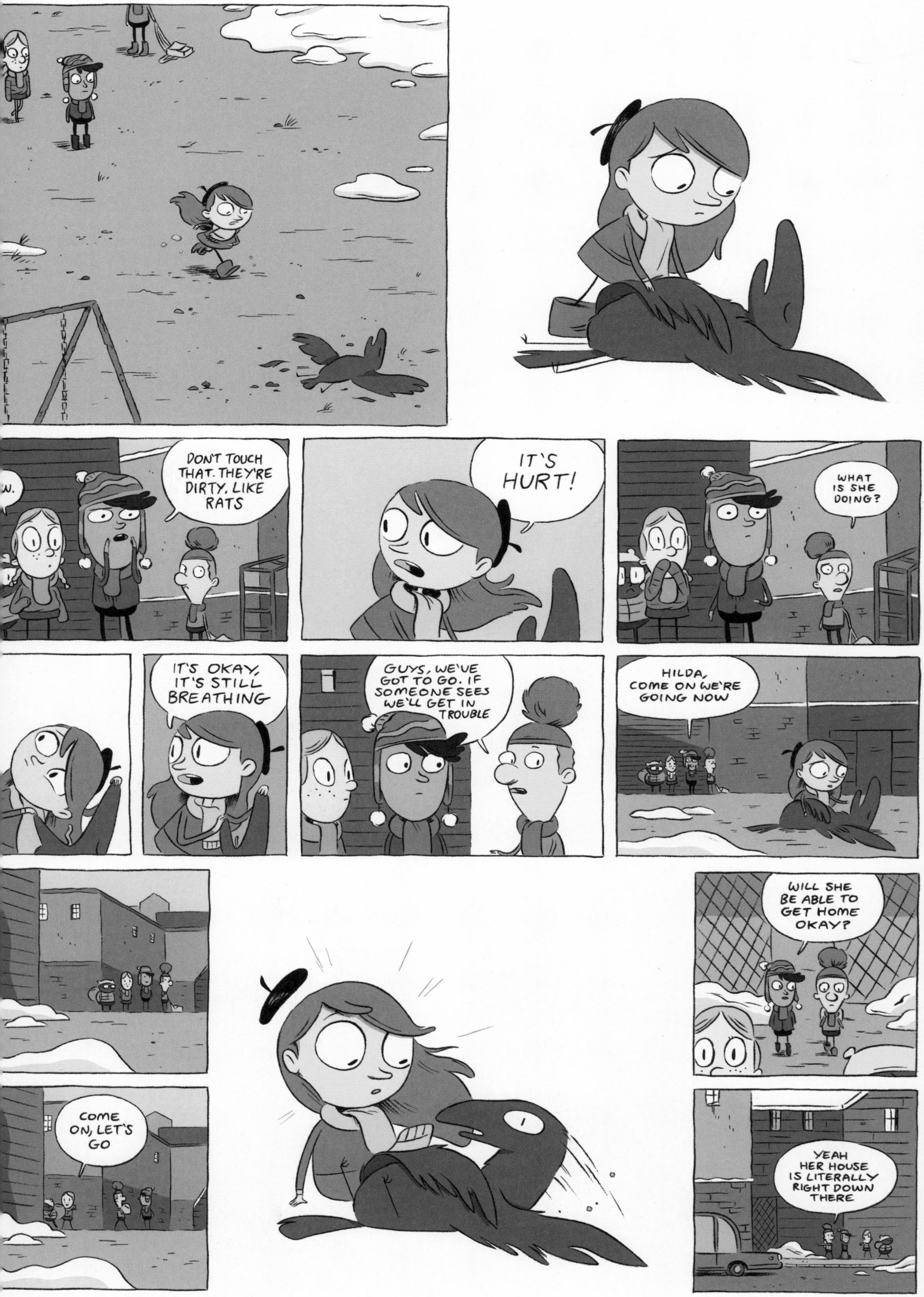
DON'T TOUCH THAT. THEY'RE DIRTY, LIKE RATS
IT'S HURT!
WHAT IS SHE DOING?
IT'S OKAY, IT'S STILL BREATHING
GUYS, WE'VE GOT TO GO. IF SOMEONE SEES WE'LL GET IN TROUBLE
HILDA, COME ON WE'RE GOING NOW
WILL SHE BE ABLE TO GET HOME OKAY?
COME ON, LET'S GO
YEAH HER HOUSE IS LITERALLY RIGHT DOWN THERE

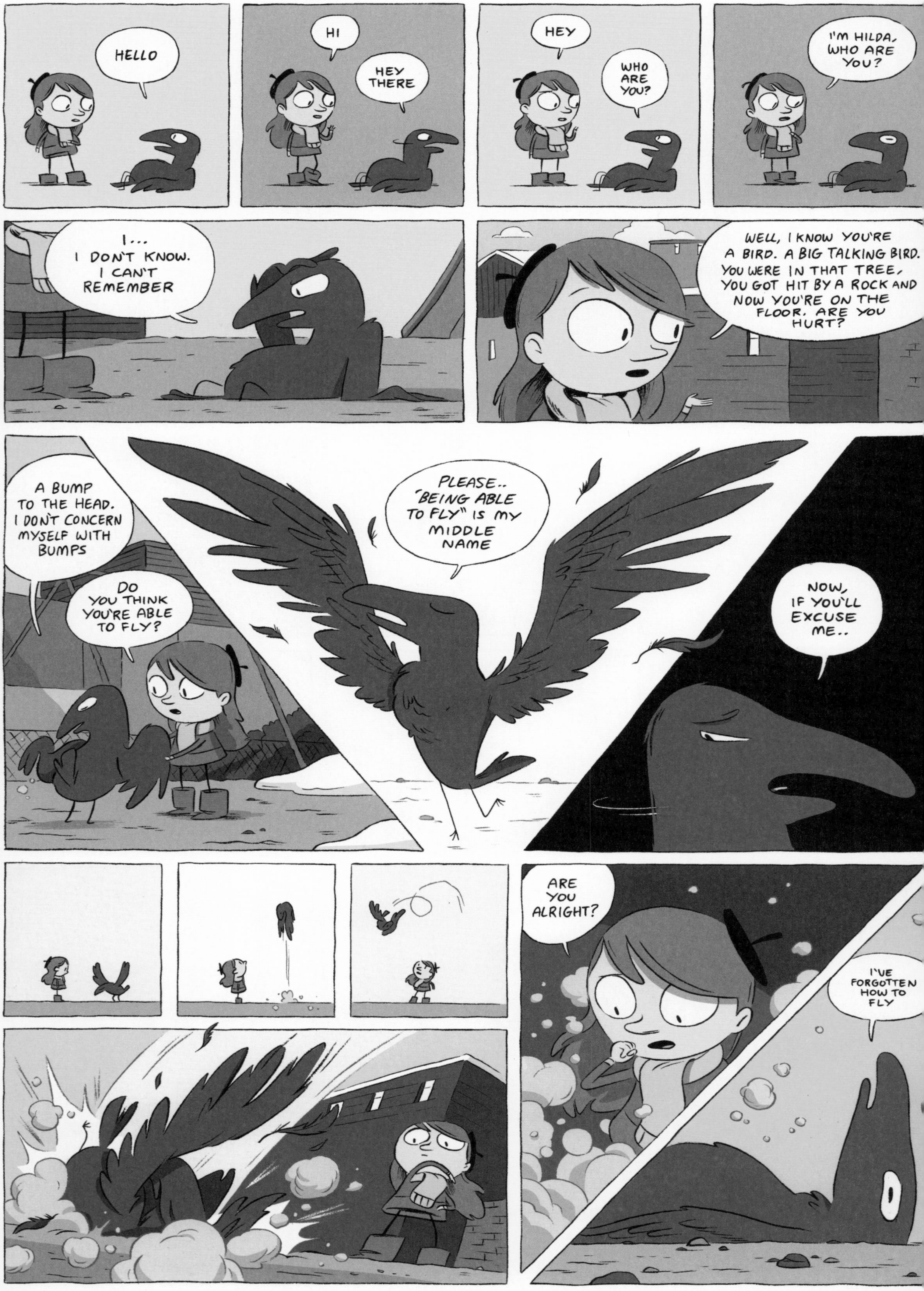
HELLO
HI
HEY THERE
HEY
WHO ARE YOU?
I'M HILDA, WHO ARE YOU?
I... I DON'T KNOW. I CAN'T REMEMBER
WELL, I KNOW YOU'RE A BIRD. A BIG TALKING BIRD. YOU WERE IN THAT TREE, YOU GOT HIT BY A ROCK AND NOW YOU'RE ON THE FLOOR. ARE YOU HURT?
A BUMP TO THE HEAD. I DON'T CONCERN MYSELF WITH BUMPS
DO YOU THINK YOU'RE ABLE TO FLY?
PLEASE.. "BEING ABLE TO FLY" IS MY MIDDLE NAME
NOW, IF YOU'LL EXCUSE ME..
ARE YOU ALRIGHT?
I'VE FORGOTTEN HOW TO FLY

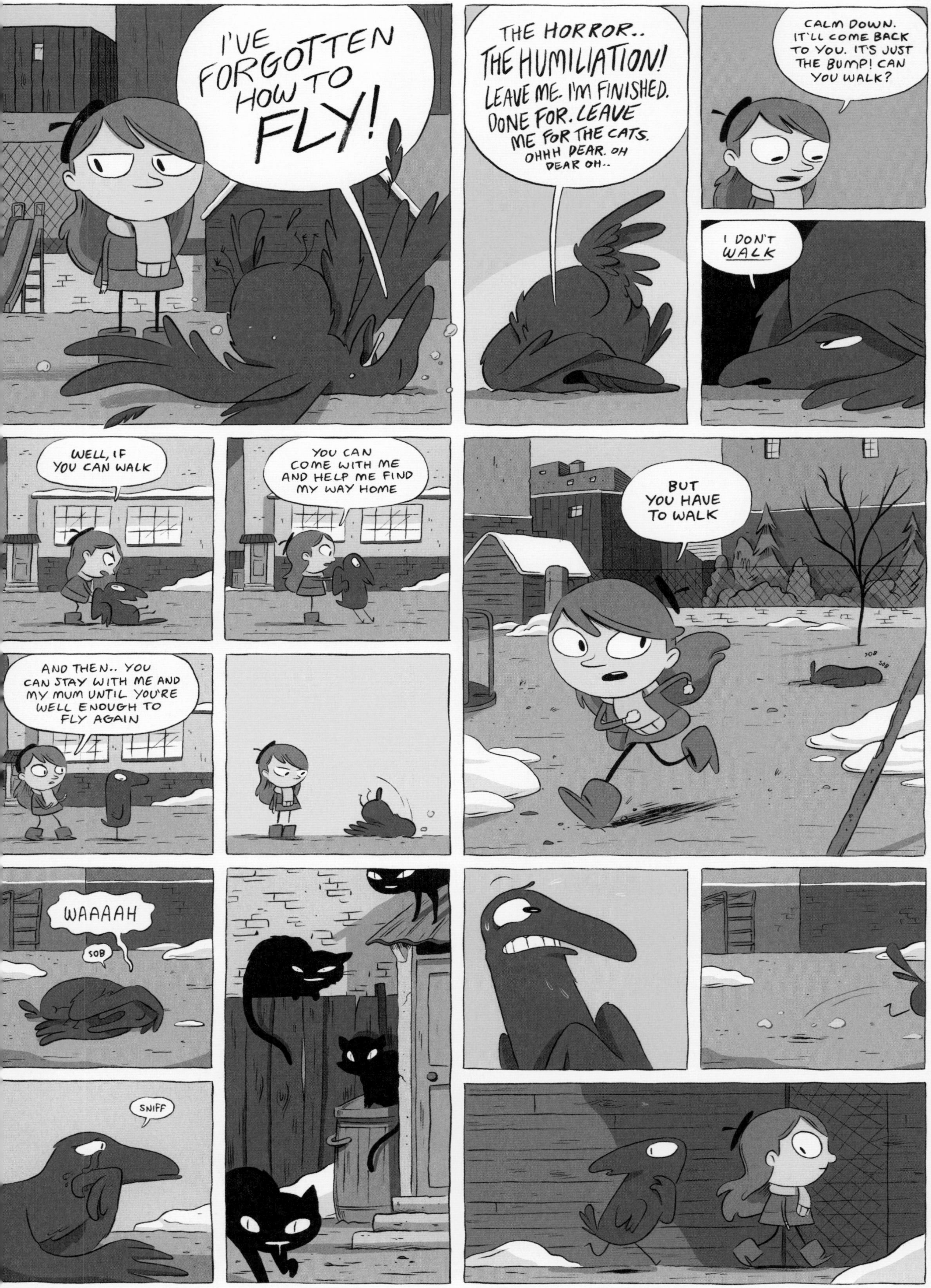

I'VE FORGOTTEN HOW TO FLY!
THE HORROR.. THE HUMILIATION! LEAVE ME. I'M FINISHED. DONE FOR. LEAVE ME FOR THE CATS. OHHH DEAR. OH DEAR OH..
CALM DOWN. IT'LL COME BACK TO YOU. IT'S JUST THE BUMP! CAN YOU WALK?
I DON'T WALK
WELL, IF YOU CAN WALK
YOU CAN COME WITH ME AND HELP ME FIND MY WAY HOME
BUT YOU HAVE TO WALK
SOB
SOB
AND THEN.. YOU CAN STAY WITH ME AND MY MUM UNTIL YOU'RE WELL ENOUGH TO FLY AGAIN
WAAAAH
SOB
SNIFF

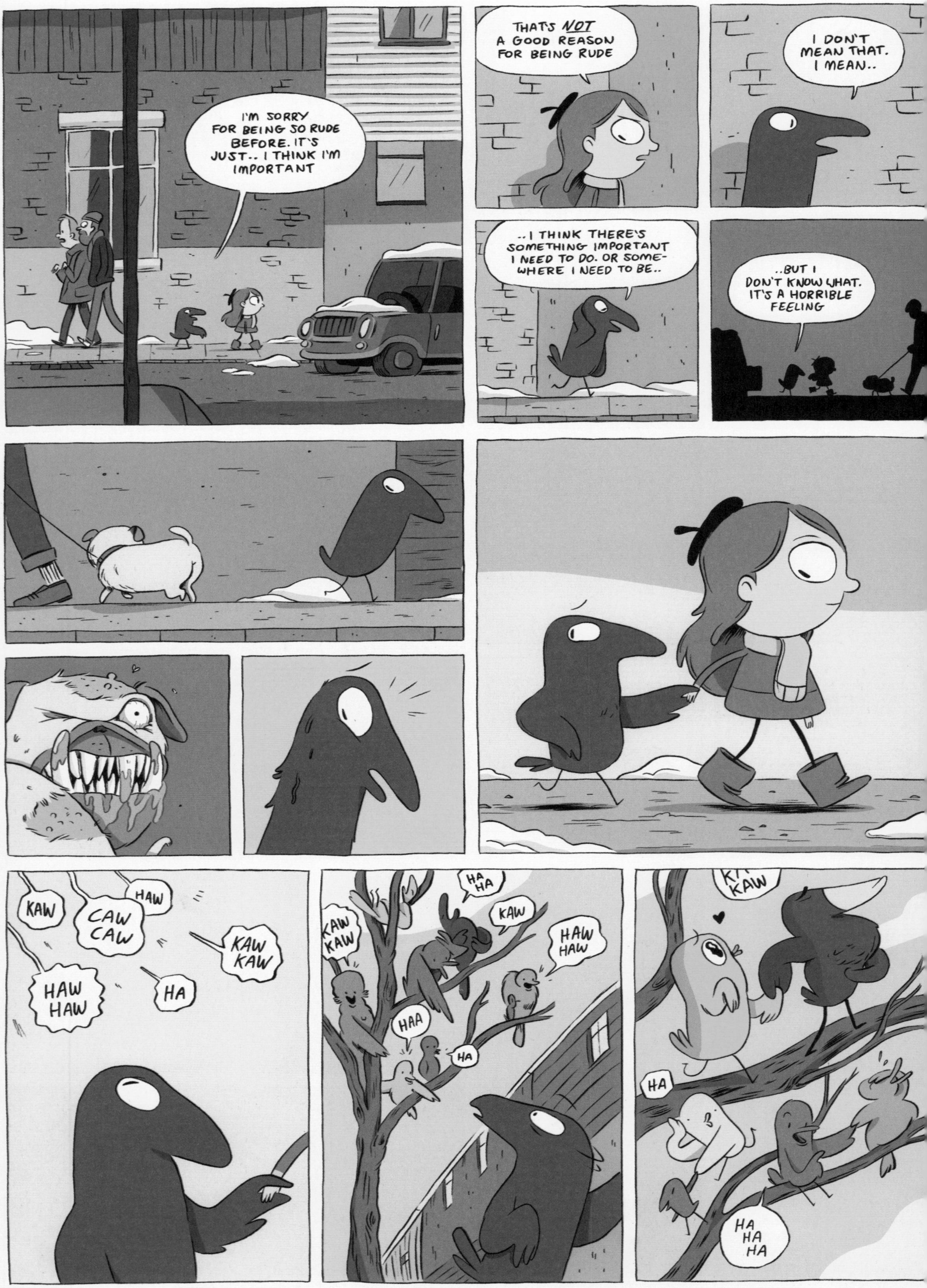
I'M SORRY FOR BEING SO RUDE BEFORE. IT'S JUST.. I THINK I'M IMPORTANT
THAT'S NOT A GOOD REASON FOR BEING RUDE
I DON'T MEAN THAT. I MEAN..
..I THINK THERE'S SOMETHING IMPORTANT I NEED TO DO. OR SOMEWHERE I NEED TO BE..
..BUT I DON'T KNOW WHAT. IT'S A HORRIBLE FEELING
KAW
CAW CAW
HAW
KAW KAW
HAW HAW
HA
KAW KAW
HA HA
KAW
HAW HAW
HAA
HA
KAW
HA
HA HA HA

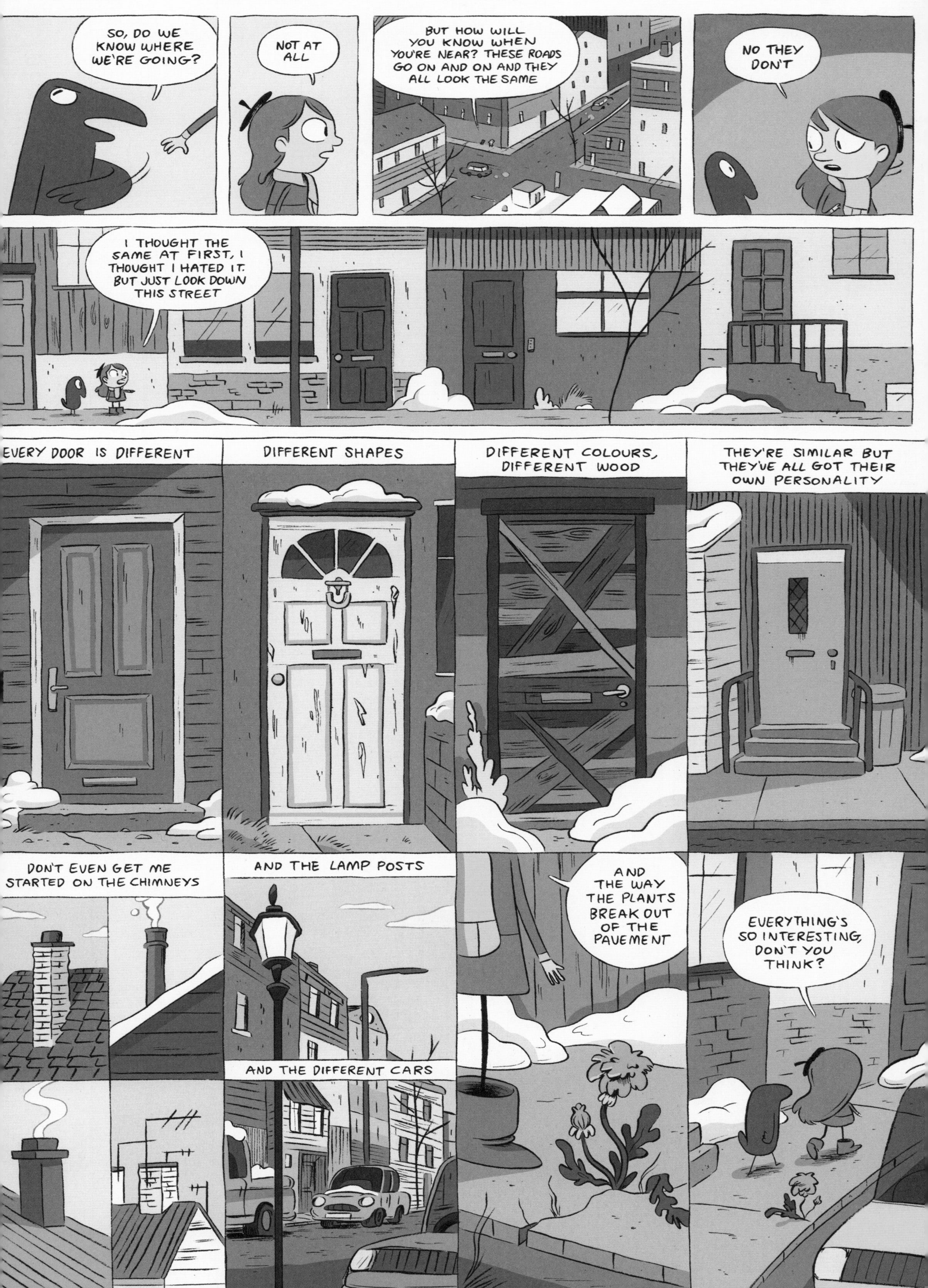
SO, DO WE KNOW WHERE WE'RE GOING?
NOT AT ALL
BUT HOW WILL YOU KNOW WHEN YOU'RE NEAR? THESE ROADS GO ON AND ON AND THEY ALL LOOK THE SAME
NO THEY DON'T
I THOUGHT THE SAME AT FIRST, I THOUGHT I HATED IT. BUT JUST LOOK DOWN THIS STREET
EVERY DOOR IS DIFFERENT
DIFFERENT SHAPES
DIFFERENT COLOURS, DIFFERENT WOOD
THEY'RE SIMILAR BUT THEY'VE ALL GOT THEIR OWN PERSONALITY
DON'T EVEN GET ME STARTED ON THE CHIMNEYS
AND THE LAMP POSTS
AND THE DIFFERENT CARS
AND THE WAY THE PLANTS BREAK OUT OF THE PAVEMENT
EVERYTHING'S SO INTERESTING, DON'T YOU THINK?

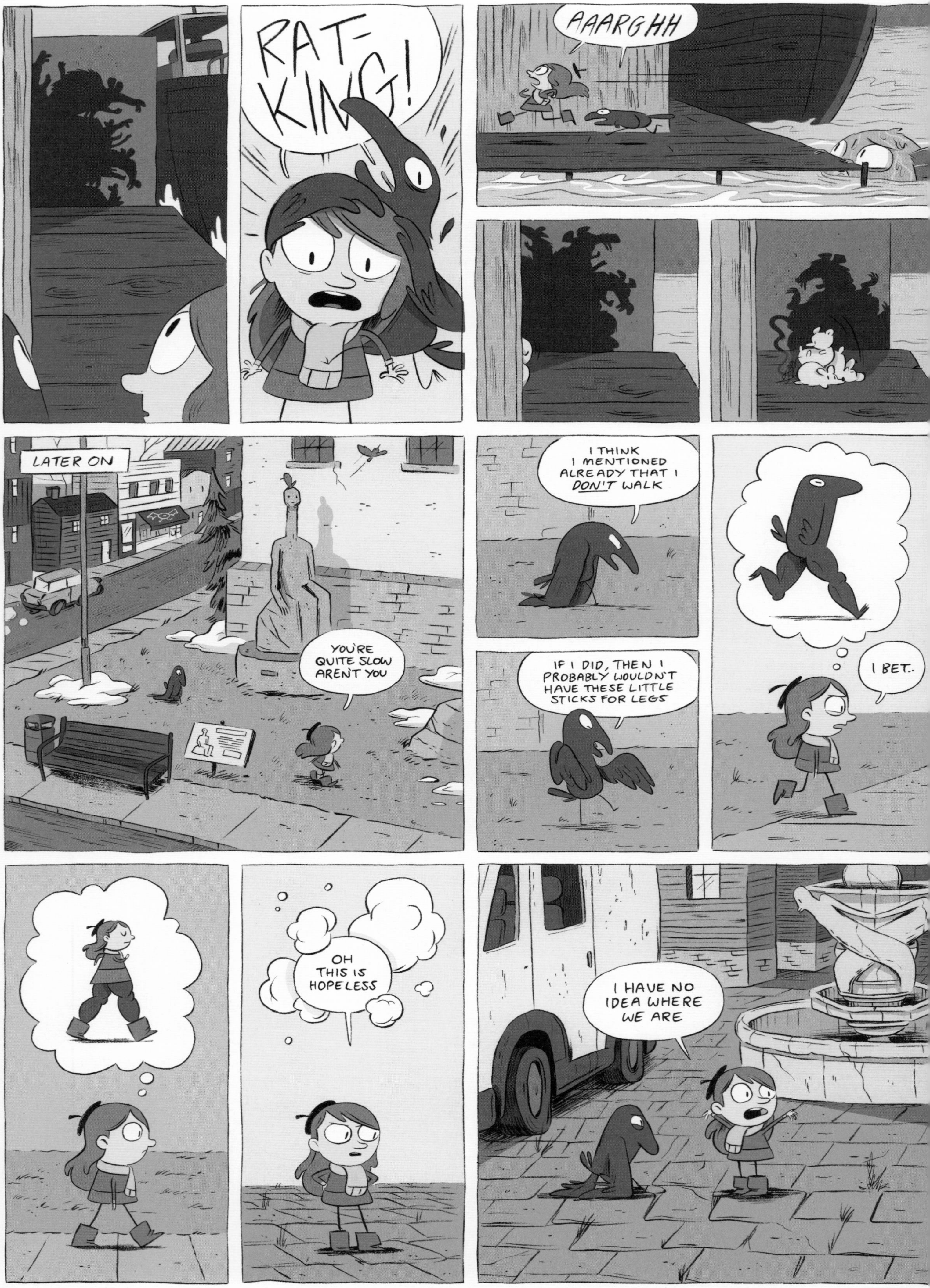
RAT-KING!
AAARGHH
LATER ON
YOU'RE QUITE SLOW AREN'T YOU
I THINK I MENTIONED ALREADY THAT I DON'T WALK
IF I DID, THEN I PROBABLY WOULDN'T HAVE THESE LITTLE STICKS FOR LEGS
I BET..
OH THIS IS HOPELESS
I HAVE NO IDEA WHERE WE ARE

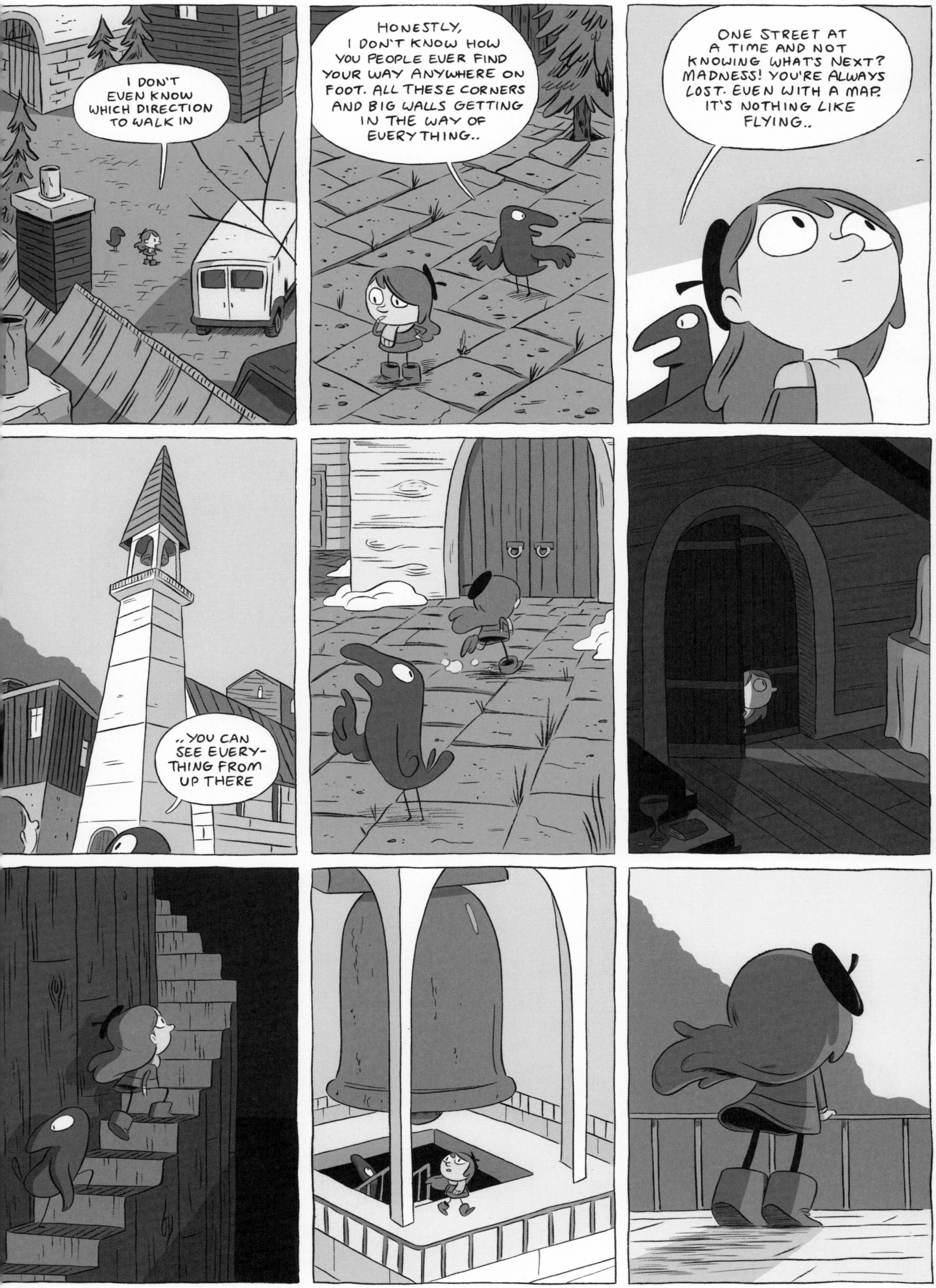
I DON'T EVEN KNOW WHICH DIRECTION TO WALK IN
HONESTLY, I DON'T KNOW HOW YOU PEOPLE EVER FIND YOUR WAY ANYWHERE ON FOOT. ALL THESE CORNERS AND BIG WALLS GETTING IN THE WAY OF EVERYTHING..
ONE STREET AT A TIME AND NOT KNOWING WHAT'S NEXT? MADNESS! YOU'RE ALWAYS LOST. EVEN WITH A MAP. IT'S NOTHING LIKE FLYING..
..YOU CAN SEE EVERY-THING FROM UP THERE

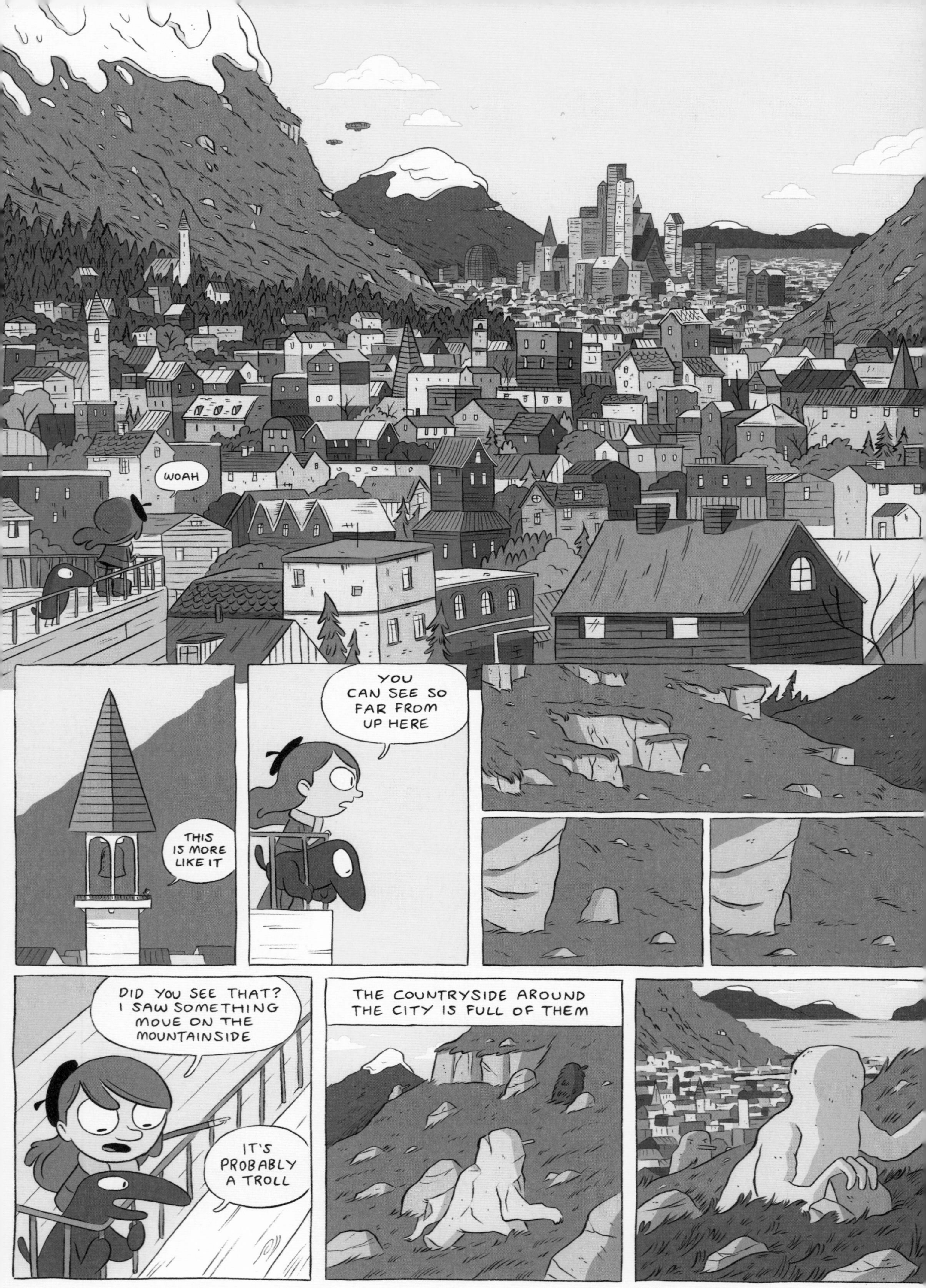
WOAH
THIS IS MORE LIKE IT
YOU CAN SEE SO FAR FROM UP HERE
DID YOU SEE THAT? I SAW SOMETHING MOVE ON THE MOUNTAINSIDE
IT'S PROBABLY A TROLL
THE COUNTRYSIDE AROUND THE CITY IS FULL OF THEM

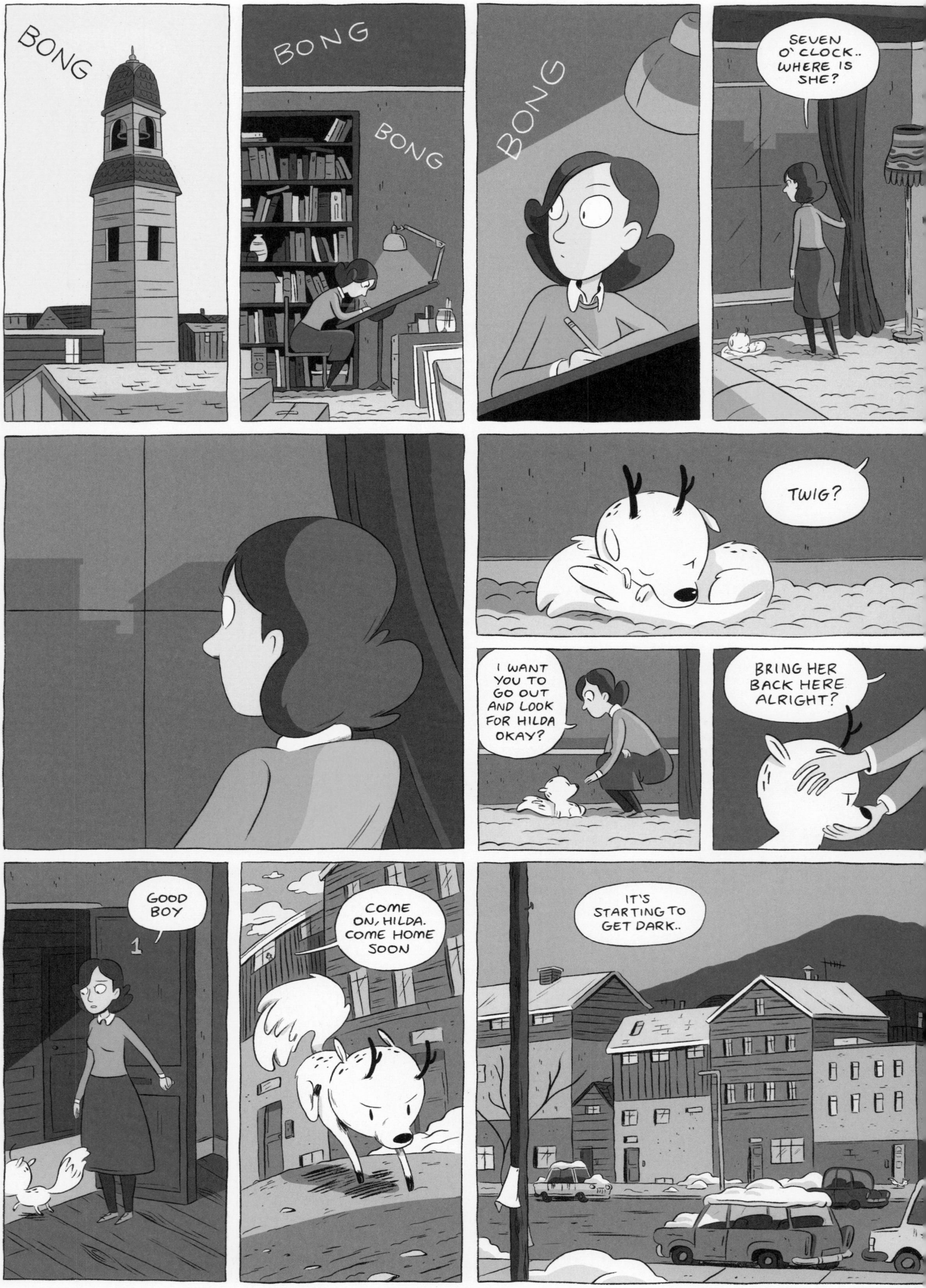
BONG
BONG
BONG
BONG
SEVEN O' CLOCK.. WHERE IS SHE?
TWIG?
I WANT YOU TO GO OUT AND LOOK FOR HILDA OKAY?
BRING HER BACK HERE ALRIGHT?
GOOD BOY
1
COME ON, HILDA. COME HOME SOON
IT'S STARTING TO GET DARK..

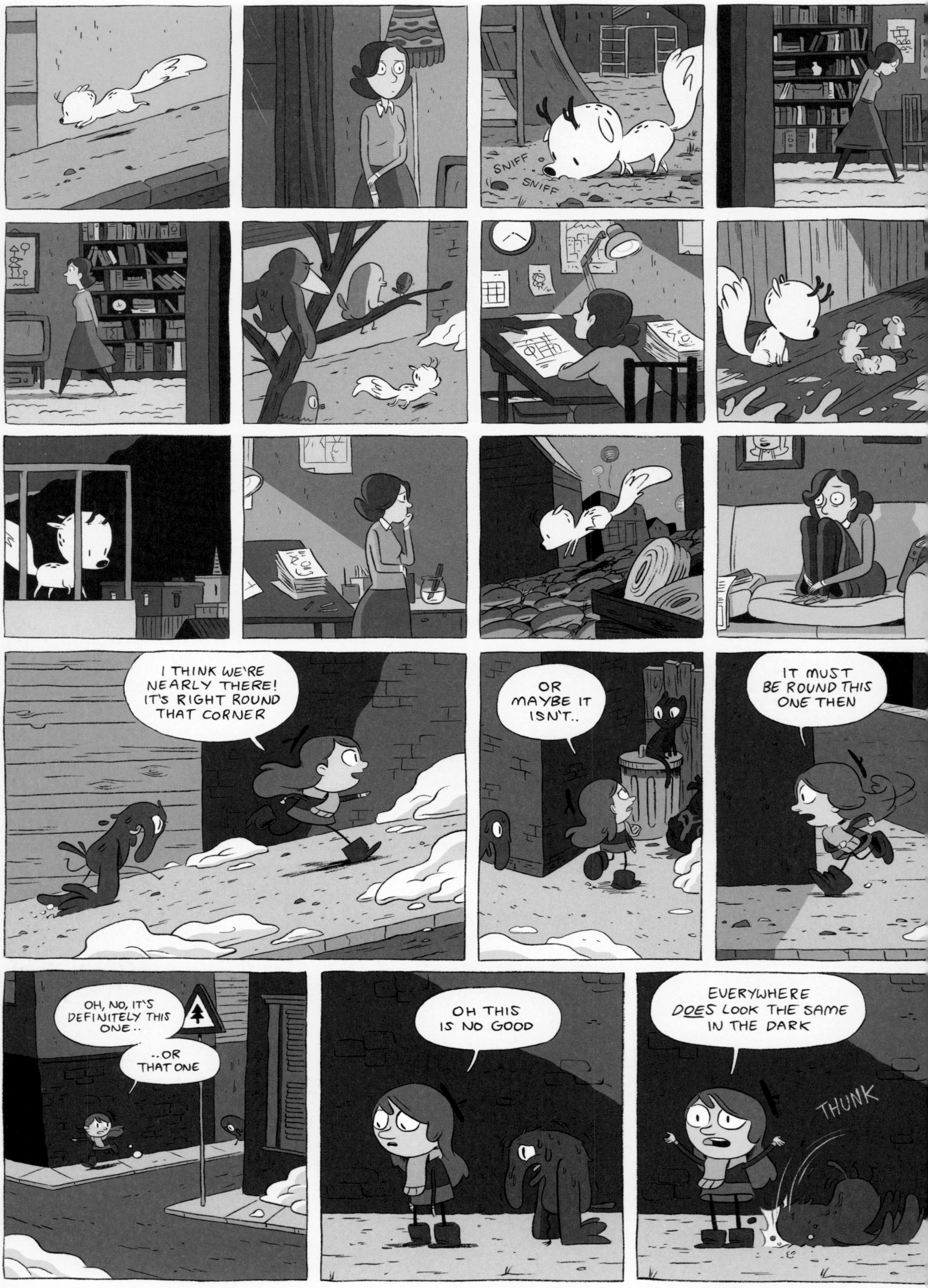
SNIFF
SNIFF
I THINK WE'RE NEARLY THERE! IT'S RIGHT ROUND THAT CORNER
OR MAYBE IT ISN'T..
IT MUST BE ROUND THIS ONE THEN
OH, NO, IT'S DEFINITELY THIS ONE..
..OR THAT ONE
OH THIS IS NO GOOD
EVERYWHERE DOES LOOK THE SAME IN THE DARK
THUNK

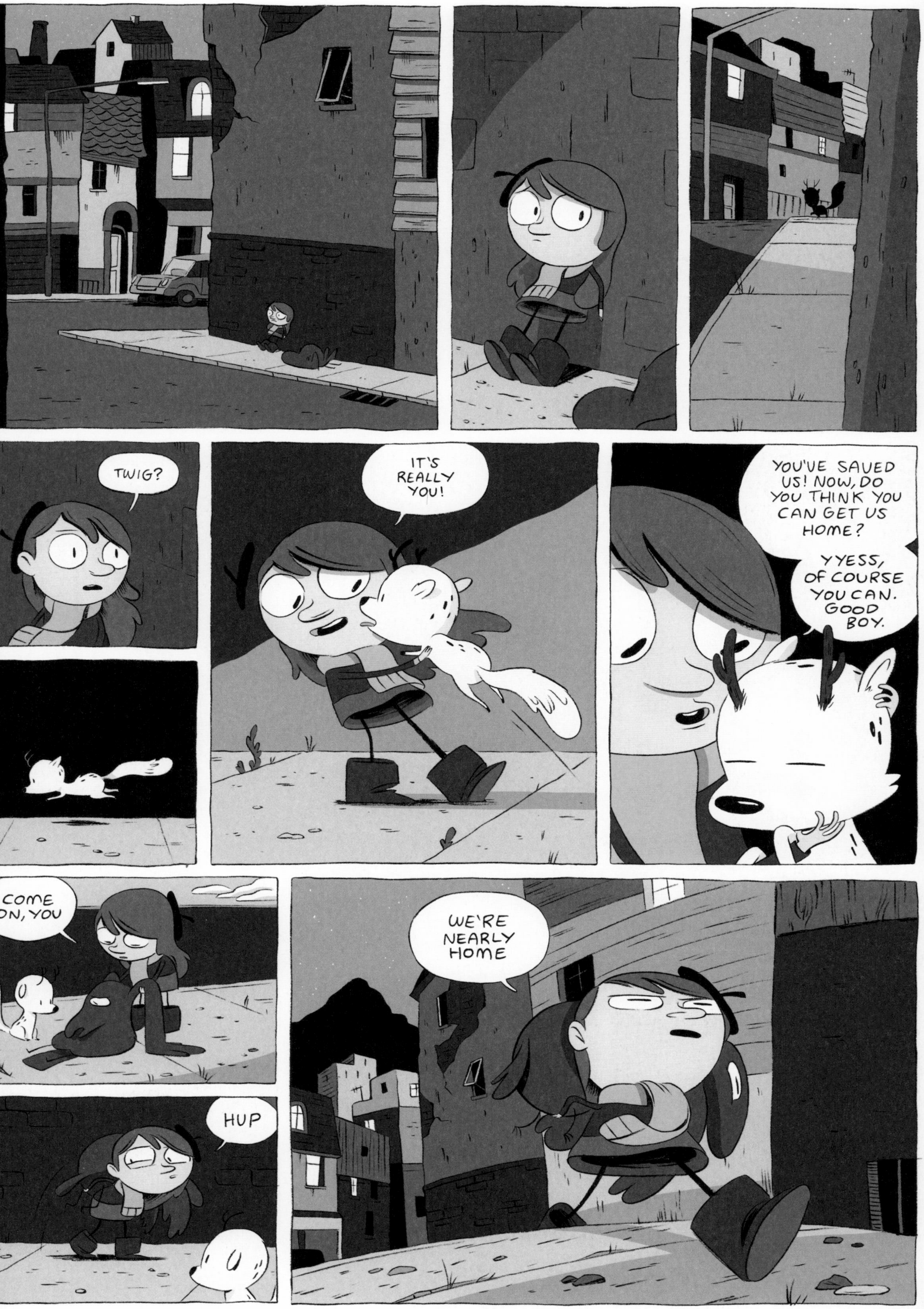

TWIG?
IT'S REALLY YOU!
YOU'VE SAVED US! NOW, DO YOU THINK YOU CAN GET US HOME?
YYESS, OF COURSE YOU CAN. GOOD BOY.
COME ON, YOU
HUP
WE'RE NEARLY HOME

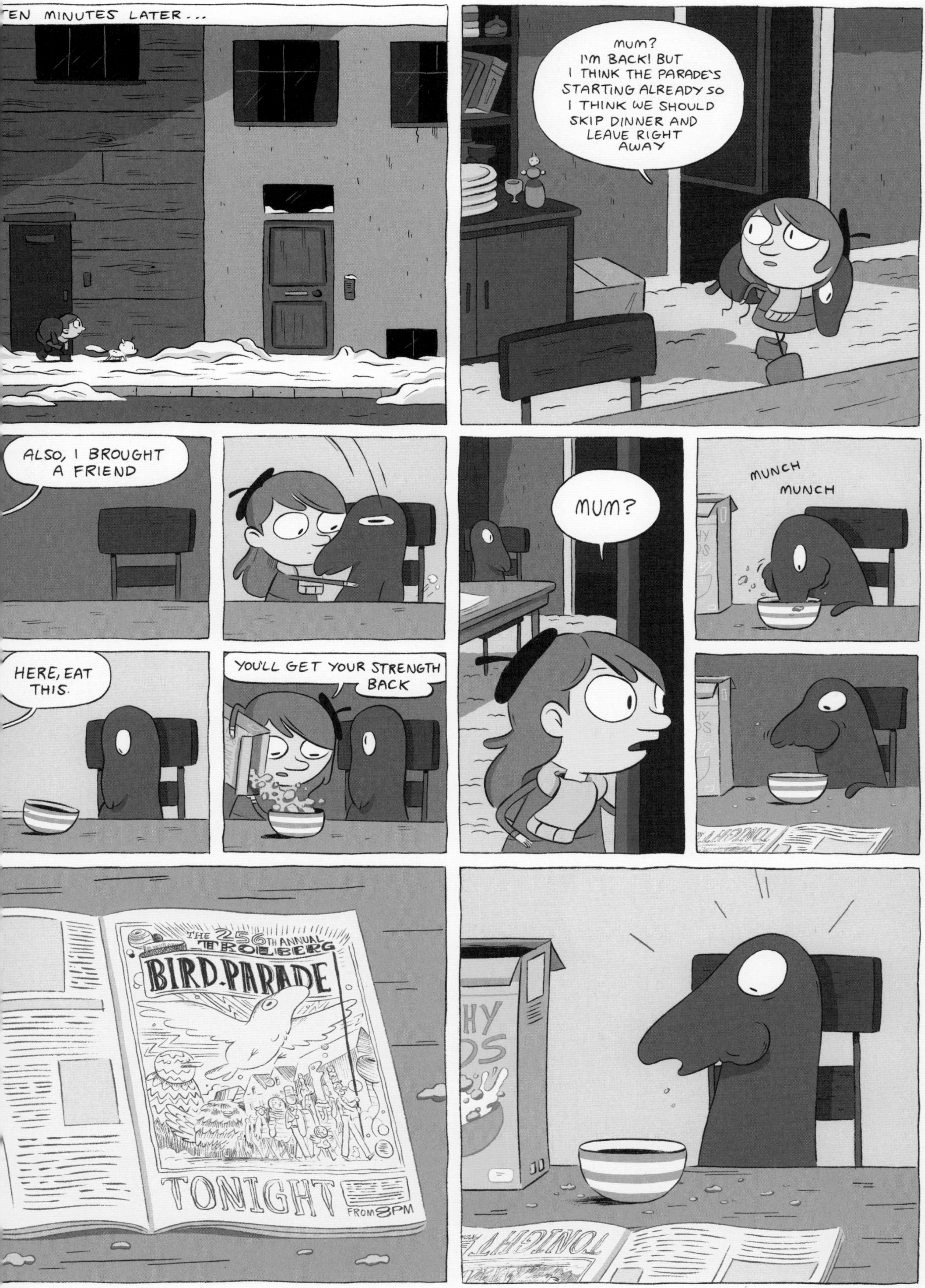
TEN MINUTES LATER...
MUM? I'M BACK! BUT I THINK THE PARADE'S STARTING ALREADY SO I THINK WE SHOULD SKIP DINNER AND LEAVE RIGHT AWAY
ALSO, I BROUGHT A FRIEND
MUM?
MUNCH
MUNCH
HERE, EAT THIS.
YOU'LL GET YOUR STRENGTH BACK
THE 256TH ANNUAL TROLBERG
BIRD PARADE
TONIGHT
FROM 8PM

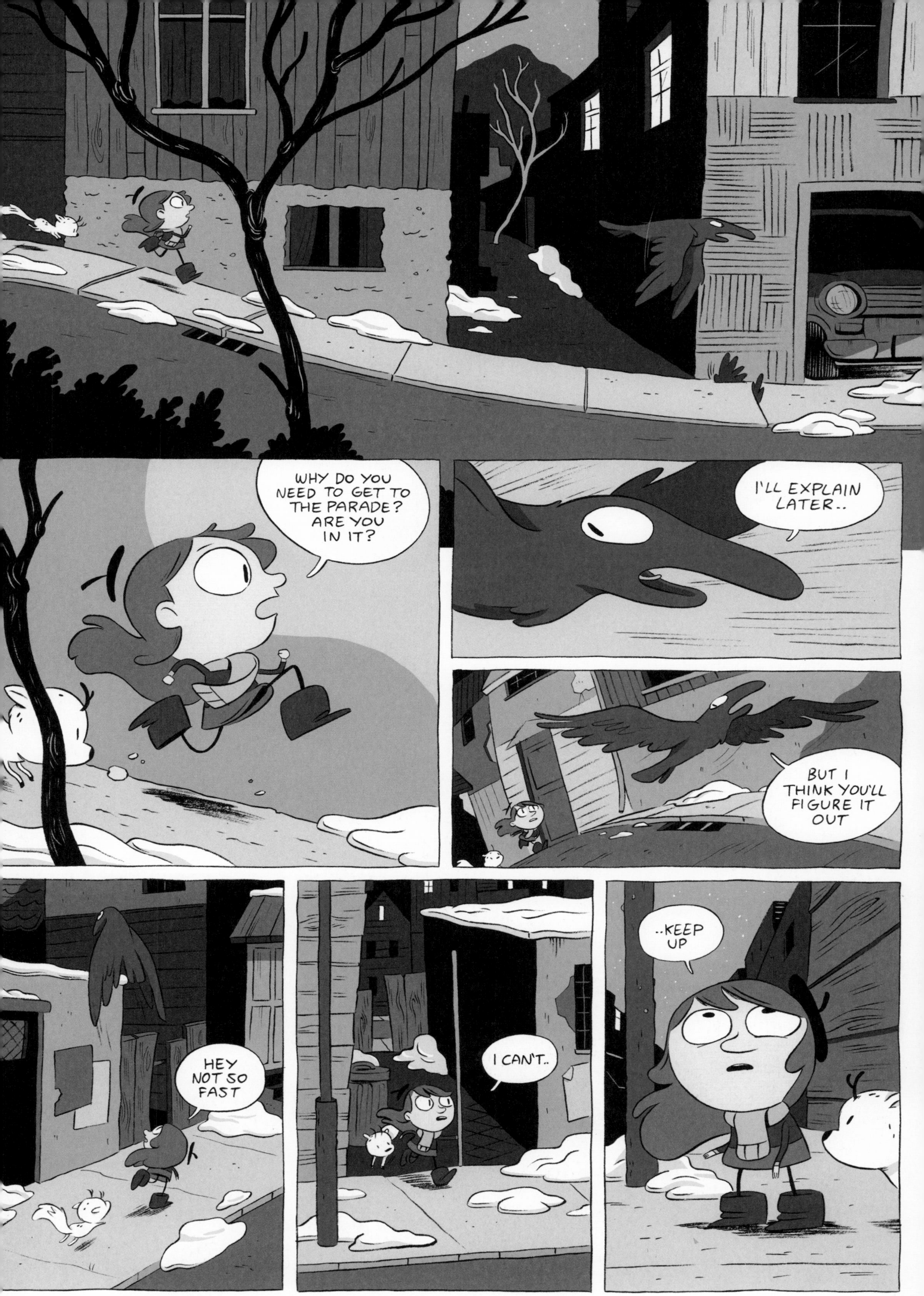
WHY DO YOU NEED TO GET TO THE PARADE? ARE YOU IN IT?
I'LL EXPLAIN LATER..
BUT I THINK YOU'LL FIGURE IT OUT
HEY NOT SO FAST
I CAN'T..
..KEEP UP

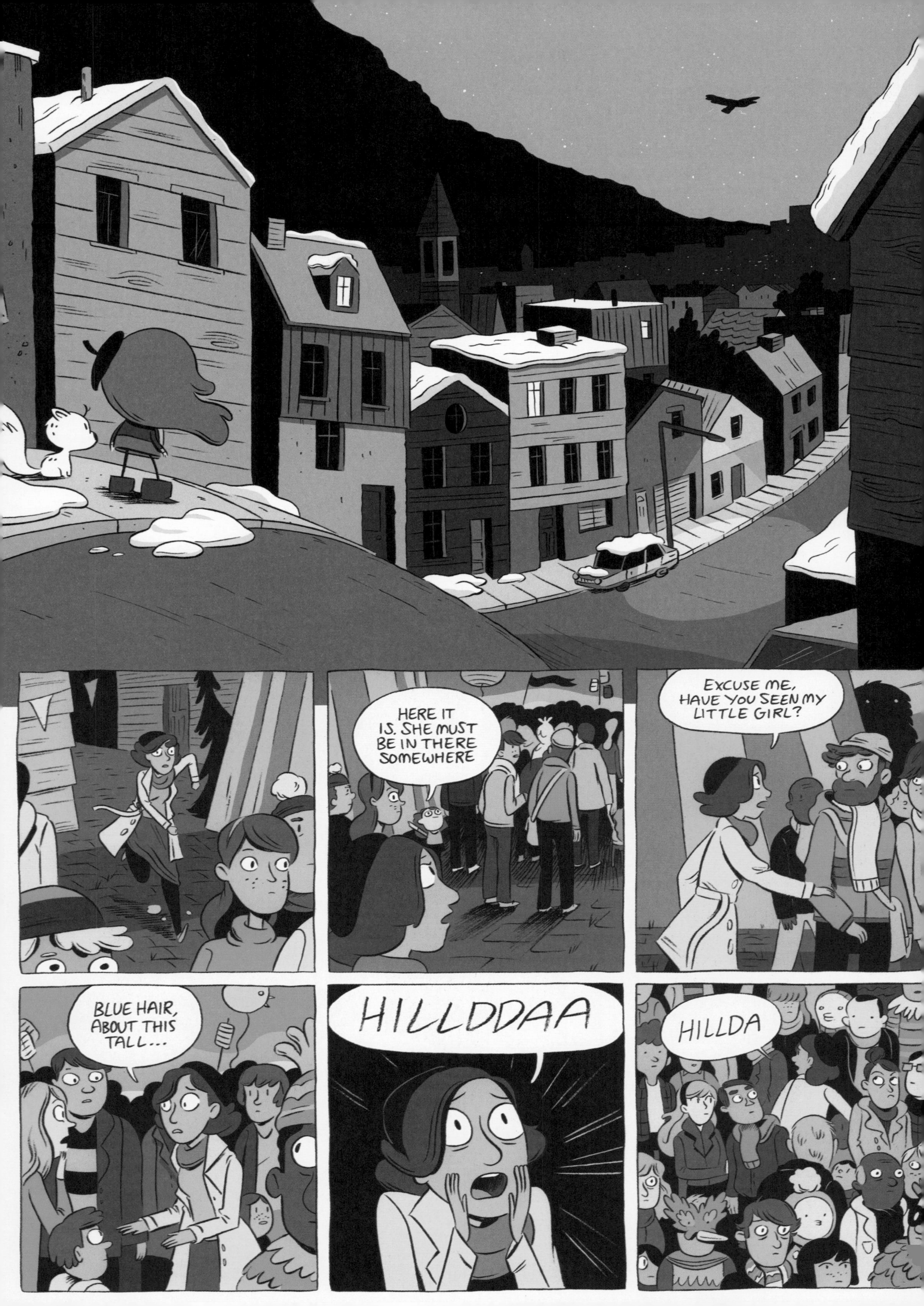
HERE IT IS. SHE MUST BE IN THERE SOMEWHERE
EXCUSE ME, HAVE YOU SEEN MY LITTLE GIRL?
BLUE HAIR, ABOUT THIS TALL...
HILLDDAA
HILLDA

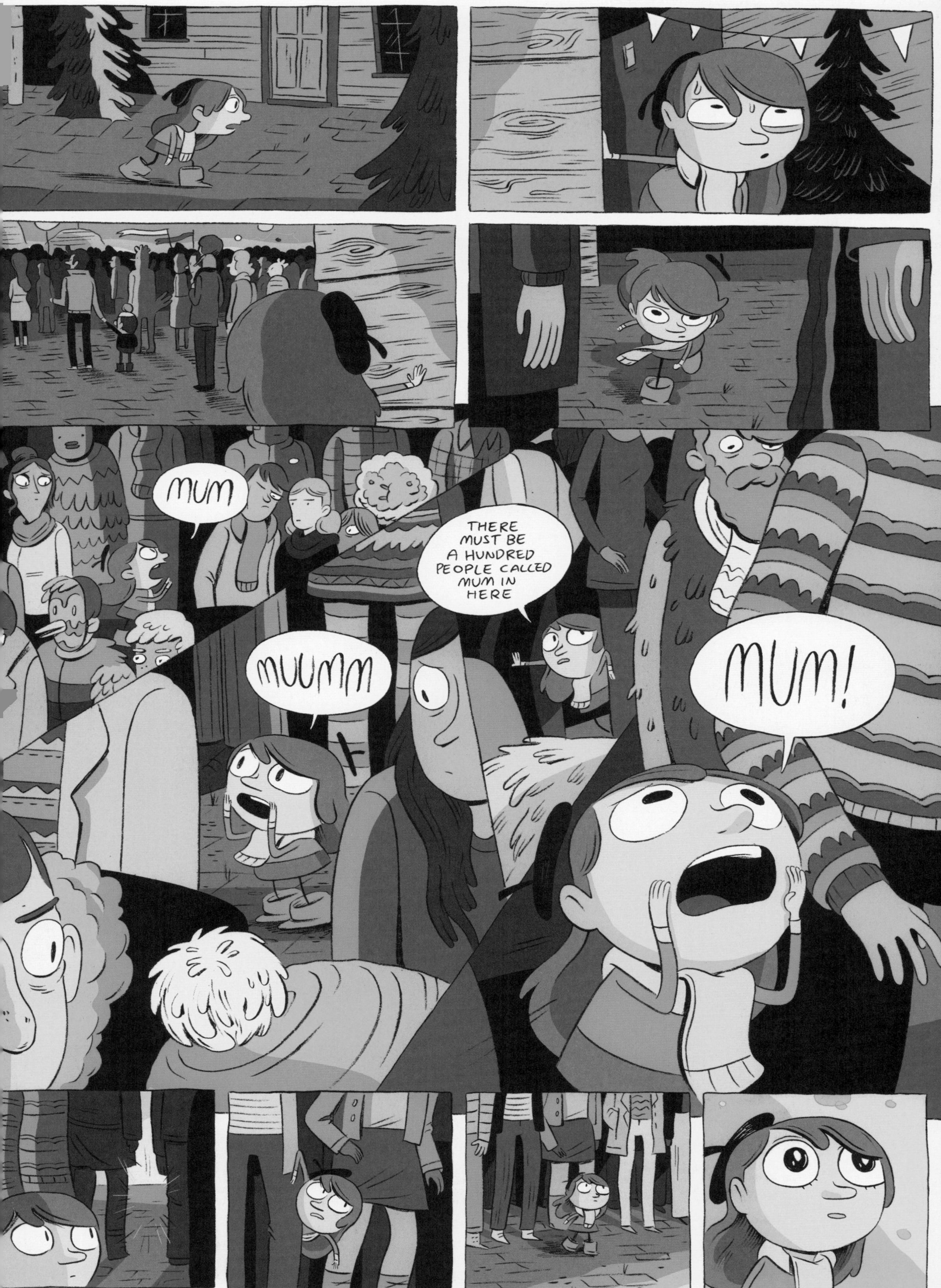
MUM
THERE MUST BE A HUNDRED PEOPLE CALLED MUM IN HERE
MUUMM
MUM!

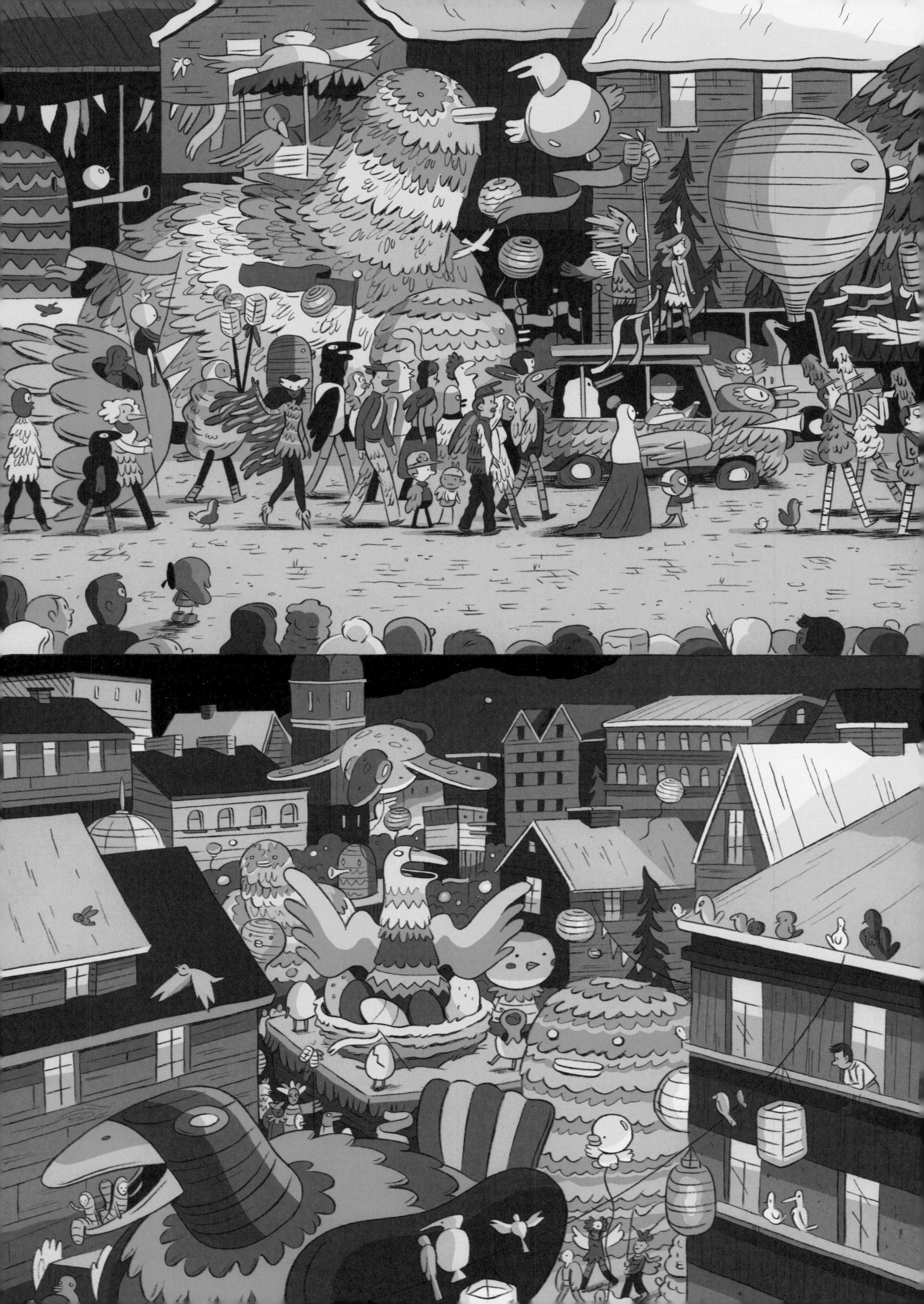

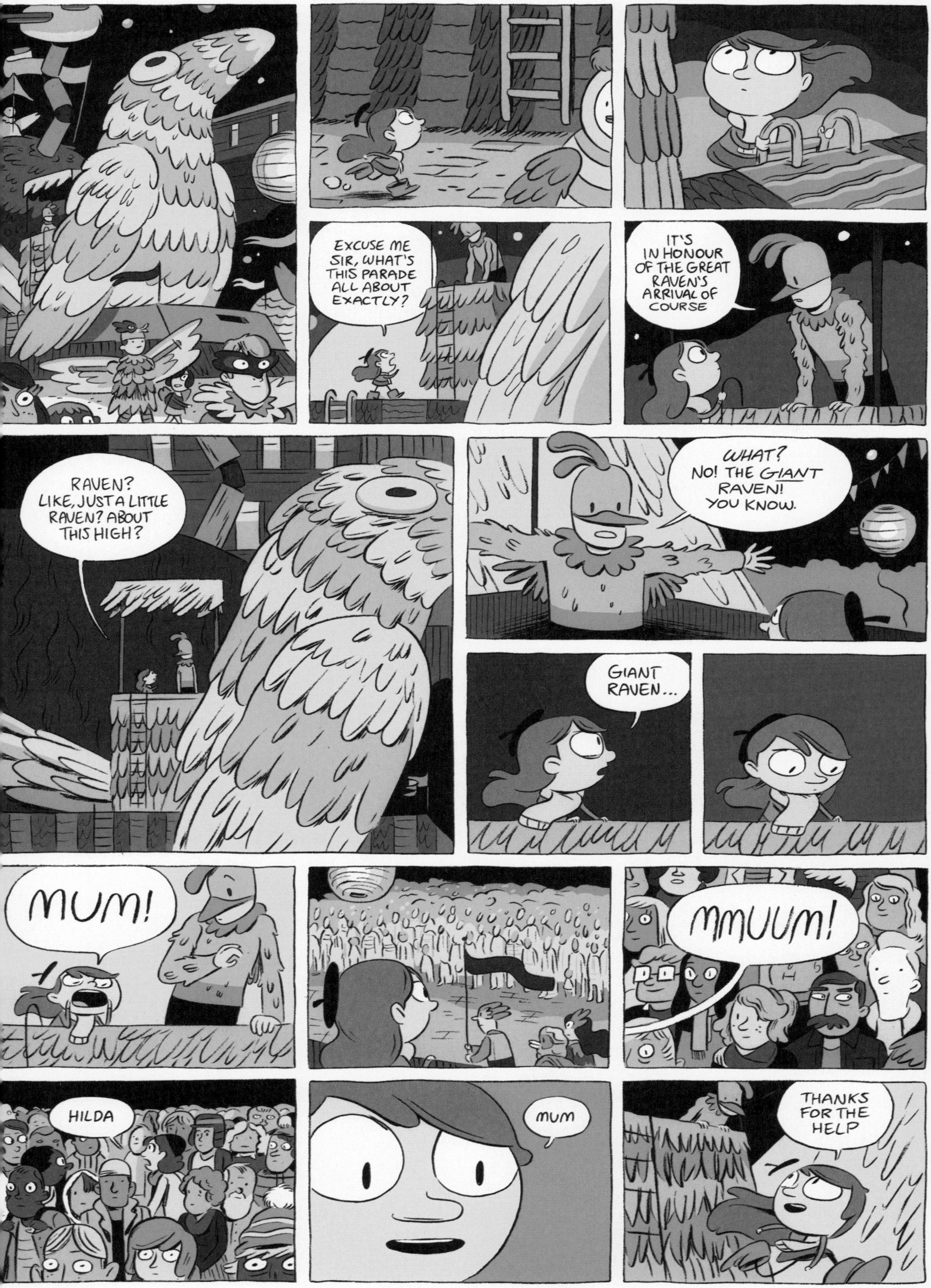
EXCUSE ME SIR, WHAT'S THIS PARADE ALL ABOUT EXACTLY?
IT'S IN HONOUR OF THE GREAT RAVEN'S ARRIVAL OF COURSE
RAVEN? LIKE, JUST A LITTLE RAVEN? ABOUT THIS HIGH?
WHAT? NO! THE GIANT RAVEN! YOU KNOW.
GIANT RAVEN...
MUM!
MMUUM!
HILDA
MUM
THANKS FOR THE HELP

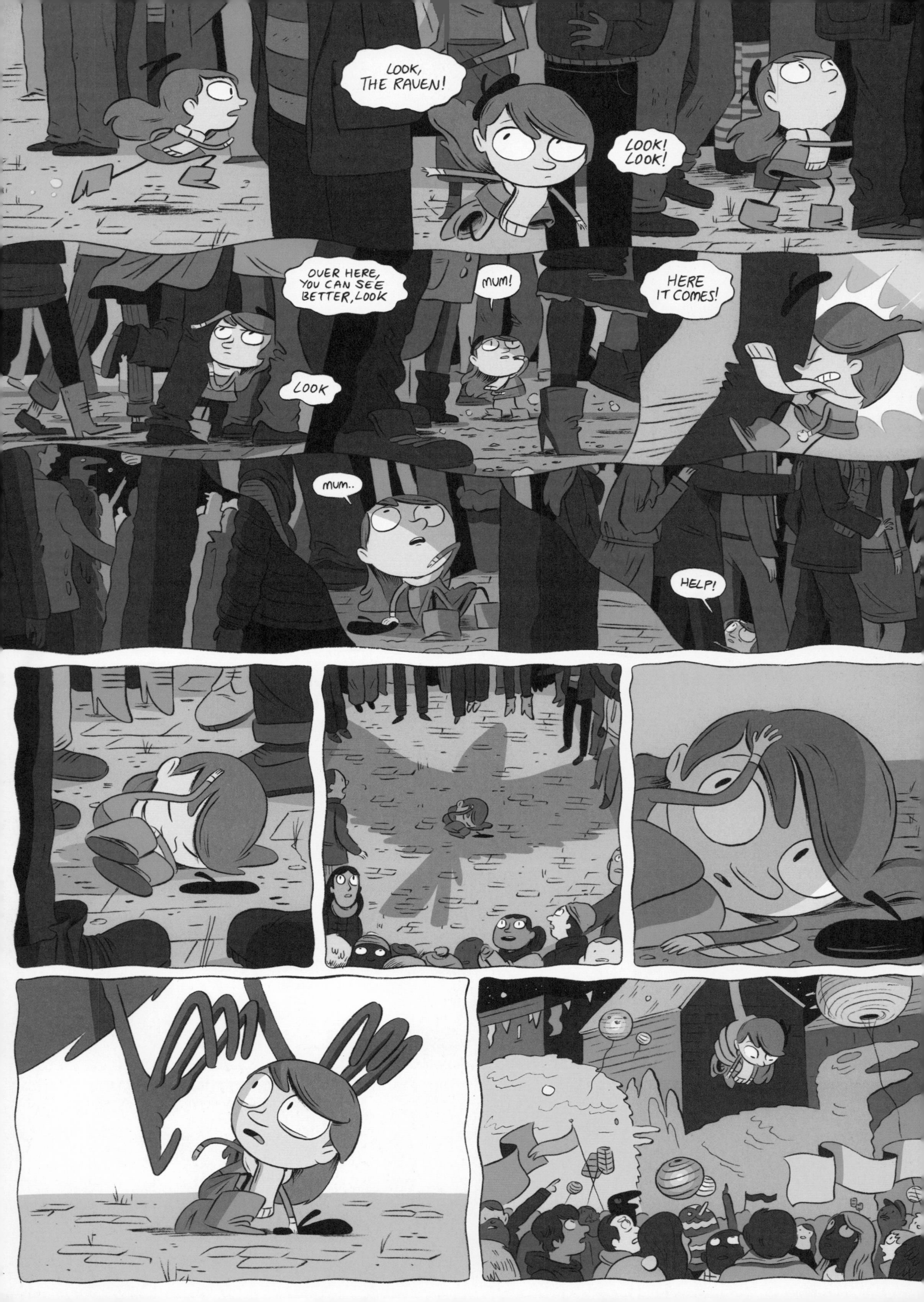
LOOK, THE RAVEN!
LOOK! LOOK!
OVER HERE, YOU CAN SEE BETTER, LOOK
LOOK
MUM!
HERE IT COMES!
MUM..
HELP!

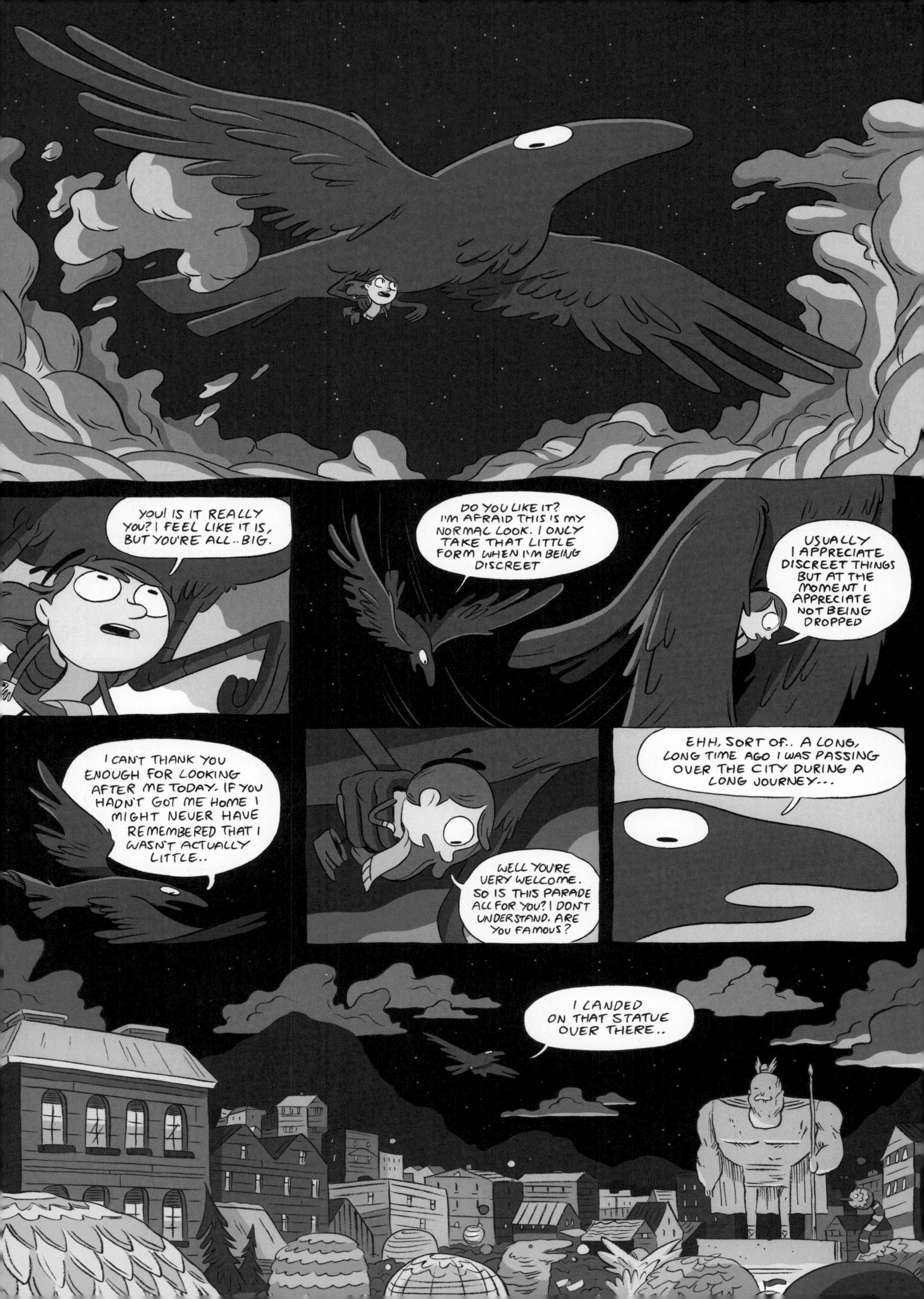
YOU! IS IT REALLY YOU? I FEEL LIKE IT IS, BUT YOU'RE ALL.. BIG.
DO YOU LIKE IT? I'M AFRAID THIS IS MY NORMAL LOOK. I ONLY TAKE THAT LITTLE FORM WHEN I'M BEING DISCREET
USUALLY I APPRECIATE DISCREET THINGS BUT AT THE MOMENT I APPRECIATE NOT BEING DROPPED
I CAN'T THANK YOU ENOUGH FOR LOOKING AFTER ME TODAY. IF YOU HADN'T GOT ME HOME I MIGHT NEVER HAVE REMEMBERED THAT I WASN'T ACTUALLY LITTLE..
WELL YOU'RE VERY WELCOME. SO IS THIS PARADE ALL FOR YOU? I DON'T UNDERSTAND. ARE YOU FAMOUS?
EHH, SORT OF.. A LONG, LONG TIME AGO I WAS PASSING OVER THE CITY DURING A LONG JOURNEY...
I LANDED ON THAT STATUE OVER THERE..

This is a second edition, printed in 2013.

Hilda and the Bird Parade is © 2012 Nobrow Ltd.

All artwork and characters within are © 2012 Nobrow Ltd. and Luke Pearson.

Published in the USA by Flying Eye Books an imprint of Nobrow Ltd.
62 Great Eastern Street, London, EC2A 3QR

Design by Sam Arthur and Alex Spiro
Printed in Belgium on FSC assured paper

ISBN: 978-1-909263-06-2

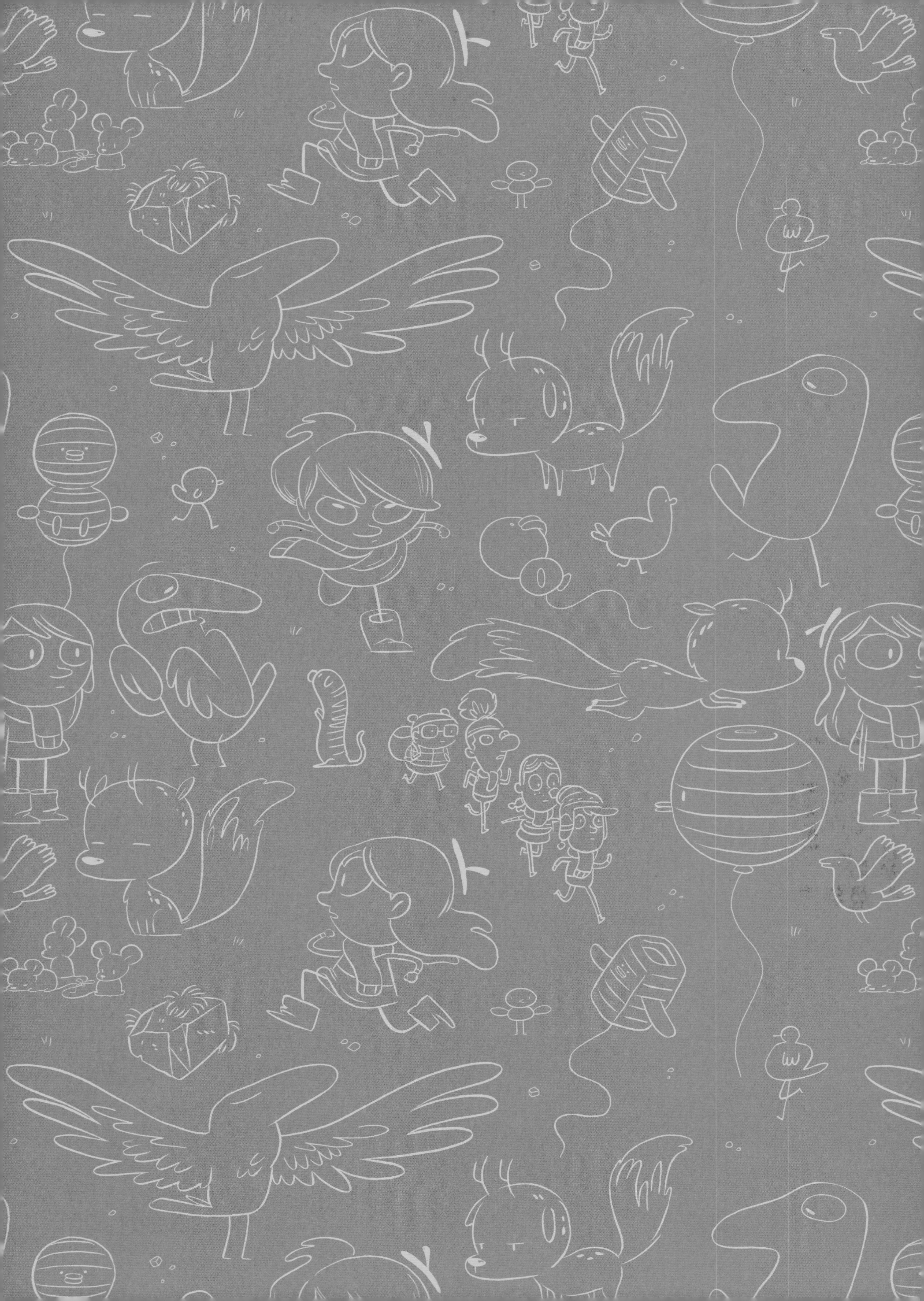